This Life

(A Murphy Brothers Story)

BY
JENNIFER RODEWALD

This Life
Copyright © 2021 Jennifer Rodewald.

ISBN: 978-1-7347421-5-2

Any references to events, real people, or real places are used fictitiously. Names, characters, and places are products of the author's imagination, and any similarities to real events are purely accidental.

Front cover image Lightstock.com. Design by Jennifer Rodewald.
First printing edition 2020.
Rooted Publishing
McCook, NE 69001

Email: jen@authorjenrodewald.com
https://authorjenrodewald.com/

MURPHY BROTHERS STORIES:

Always You

Inspite of Ourselves

Everything Behind Us

This Life

Stubborn Love

Praise be to you, Lord,
the God of our father Israel,
from everlasting to everlasting.
Yours, Lord, is the greatness and the power
and the glory and the majesty and the splendor,
for everything in heaven and earth is yours.
Yours, Lord, is the kingdom;
you are exalted as head over all.
Wealth and honor come from you;
you are the ruler of all things.
In your hands are strength and power
to exalt and give strength to all.
Now, our God, we give you thanks,
and praise your glorious name.

1 Chronicles 29:11–13

ThisBoondockingLife entry #52

> *I think it's time that I am honest with you.*
>
> *Unlike so many who are out there living like we are, we didn't choose this life. Steady yourselves—I know that's a shock. But it's the truth.*
>
> *The thing is, sometimes God strips you of everything, leaving you helpless, void, and wildly disillusioned. Suddenly you look around and nothing—and I do mean nothing—is where it was supposed to be. Everything has been sifted and your hands are empty.*
>
> *That is where This Boondocking Life began.*

Chapter One

(in which the emptiness is too heavy)

The emptiness had weight. Solid, sinking, and familiar. Kate Murphy hated it. And yet the vast granite bleakness remained ever present in her life. More so, as ever, when that trailer came into view.

Winter's chill had given way to the muddiness of early spring, leaving the entrance to the trailer park as a warning for what lay ahead. An ugly, sinking mess in which no one actually *wanted* to live. But some just did. Like her mother—and herself, when there hadn't been another option.

Home not-so-sweet home (no longer, and hallelujah) filled the view beyond Kate's luxury SUV windshield, and she pulled in to park in front of the 1971 ten-by-sixty trailer, the rippling brown siding and sagging red-stained skirt a clear memory Kate wished she didn't have. She'd hated being trailer trash. Hated that no matter how many jobs her mom took on, one way or another the promised "nest egg for a better life" would somehow be lost. Usually at the nearest lottery vender or keno provider.

Even now as Kate carefully stepped her Burberry-booted feet out of her new Land Rover, cringing as the rubber soles sank into the black muck of the ground, she felt the lava of shame creep through her being at having once claimed this as home. As she placed both feet firmly in the goo and shut the car door, lest the fine leather become tainted with the sludge of this life, Kate inhaled a steadying breath. She made the mistake of shutting her eyes, leaving smell as the predominate sensory receptor. The foul breath she'd drawn was one of rotting wood and leaves, poignantly mixed with a definitive odor made possible by one of the twenty trailers in the park (or likely, more than one) whose septic had been sorrowfully neglected.

Everything about this life was foul. Though she'd escaped it, Kate still hated it.

Kate lifted a hand, her fingers curving over her nose as she blinked the murky reflections of her childhood back into focus. It was too late though—the deep-set memories had begun to replay in her mind, and once started, there was little she could do to stop them.

As a girl, she hadn't known different. The trees among which she and her neighbors dwelled had been her kingdom, and she had little care that the home she and Mom shared wasn't much more than a tin can. That blissful ignorance changed when, on a fanciful whim, her mother took her to tour a model home in Sugar Pine, the nicer town across the Sugar Creek bridge. The show house had been spacious, with crystal-clear windows one could peer through without squinting. Wood floors gleamed, along with pristine countertops and bathroom fixtures that lacked the green-and-brown buildup of whatever caused those awful stains. As she'd left that vision of prosperity, discontentment had lodged in Kate's heart, along with the stinging, putrid grip of shame.

Mom must have felt it too, because from that moment forward, when Kate had been twelve, Mom swore they would move up in life. Out of the mudhole that was Sugar Creek Cove. Out of trailer-trash life. For several years, Kate had believed her. Enough that when she started working at the corner convenience store at an age that was much too young, she gave more than 90 percent of her earnings to her mother for their Moving-Up Fund.

Two other events further demolished Kate's childhood ignorance-induced contentment. The first was a fallout with her best friend, Macy, when she was fourteen. Macy had been the only friend ever allowed to hang out with Kate at Sugar Creek Cove. (Now Kate understood why parents hadn't let their sweet, affluent daughters spend time in the trailer park). With a fierce campaign of disgrace after their disagreement, Macy made known to all of Sugar Creek High the lowliness of Kate's life. Humiliation hadn't seemed the right word for it—for the ensuing weeks had felt like a slow, torturous death.

And then there was Mother's betrayal nearly a year after Macy's. On a binge that wasn't necessarily normal but wasn't uncommon either, Kate's Mom confessed that she'd lost it. All of it. Their Moving-Up Fund was gone. Gambled away on a bet inspired by the promise of 2.6 million dollars in winnings. Just guess the right numbers, and instant prosperity could be theirs...

Mother had not guessed the right numbers at all, and three years of Kate's faithful contributions to their future were gone. All of it.

In her dark misery, Kate had confided to a counselor at school all that made her feel worthless and stuck. Right or wrong, that lady recommended a change of schools. Kate could transfer over to Sugar Pine High School, just across the river and up the bend from the smaller Sugar Creek schools, and there she could begin again.

It had been a fateful move, one that rerouted her life.

Even still, Kate found herself back in Sugar Creek Cove again, feet sucked deep into the muck. Truthfully, though she'd gained the life and status she'd been after all those years back, Kate couldn't say that life was much better. If the aching discontentment in her heart was any indication at all, and surely it must be, Kate's life still reeked like the trailer park.

The pang within quivered—the move seismic—releasing pain over her heart. Though there were things she'd done back then that she wished she hadn't, Kate had never expected to live in a hollowness like this. Not ever. Jacob had been her salvation, and for just a minute they had been happy together. Hadn't they?

Swallowing against the sting, Kate shook her head and shoved a stopper into the breach of emotions. Today she was there to visit her mother, as she did every month. All the other sharp fragments of her life could keep for later—or better yet, could just keep, never to be disturbed. She could go on pretending. She and Jacob both could.

Kate brushed up her lips until she felt certain they molded into a convincing smile, pulled up first one booted foot and then another, each step making a *schluuppp* sound as the muck resentfully released the rubber soles, and strode to the narrow, rickety steps that would thrust her into the world of her past. Once inside, she removed her feet from those $500 mud boots, reminding herself that the rubber soles would indeed wash clean, and left them on the cracked olive-green linoleum entryway, the whole of which was less than three foot square.

"That my beauty queen?" Mom's voice crackled from the sagging mauve recliner, whose back faced the narrow front door and whose front was squared with the out-of-place large flat-screen television monopolizing the far end wall. Not surprisingly, some talking know-it-all jabbered on, filling Mother's head with the wisdom that apparently only celebrities could own. Bless them for divvying it out as they did, one thirty-minute segment at a time. If only every American would sit glued to their media as Mother did, prosperity and joy would be for the taking. Just look at the evidence in front of her.

Kate rolled her eyes and marched to the much-too-large screen, snapping the power button on the side.

"Hey, I was learning stuff there." Mom leaned forward but didn't move farther than that. Her feet, covered in filthy slippers that had been worn indoors, outdoors, and everywhere else for the past year, remained propped up on the recliner's footstool. "Might best you flip that thing back on, little miss richy-pants. I'm still your mother."

"Mom, it's nearly noon, and you're still in bed clothes."

"Bed clothes, is they?" Mom snorted. "Us plain folk call 'em jammies, Your Highness. And it's Tuesday."

Tuesday. Kate wanted to roll her eyes. A nonsensical statement to the normal world. But for Mother, it could be any day. It wouldn't matter.

"You promised, Mom."

"I looked, baby girl. There ain't no jobs to suit."

Meaning there wasn't anyone willing to pay her to sit there and watch talk shows. Shocking.

Kate sighed. At one point, her mother had actually held down two jobs at once. They hadn't been glamorous. She'd been a janitor for a little church that hosted a preschool, an evening gig. And she'd worked at a filling station at the crossroads of Sugar Creek and Sugar Pine during the day. That had been back when they had hopes and dreams and a salt's worth of ambition. Things that flushed away (with shocking speed) with the insane conviction that the lottery was some sort of salvation for the poor and Jacob Murphy was God's appointed financial float until that deliverance was revealed.

"Where's Rodney?" Kate asked.

Mom held a haughty stare, her lips pursed for a moment before she chose to answer. "Down at the Creekside."

Of course he was. The Creekside grill and pub was the nearest keno provider.

"Mom..."

"Look, you should know better than to stand in judgment. We do what we gotta do. At least Rodney's disability covers some bills."

Right. The disability that wasn't legitimate, and yes, it could cover some bills if they actually paid them. Kate met her mother's defiant look with a rising anger. "I got a call from the Cove. Again, Mother."

Mom simply looked to the side, her mouth shifting, as if she were trying to decide what to eat rather than acknowledge the complaint Kate had laid down.

"Rodney's disability should have covered the lease. And the electricity." Kate folded her arms. "And frankly, everything else. That doesn't even account for the money I gave you last month. Mom, it was nearly fifteen hundred dollars. What did you do with it?"

"That ain't none of your business, missy."

"It was *my* money!"

"No t'weren't. You gave it. My name was on the check and all."

Kate stared at the woman incredulously. More amazing than her mother's twisted thinking was the fact that hearing it surprised Kate. Again. How could she still be shocked by this?

"Mom." Kate twisted her hands together, stepped to the poop-brown recliner that had moved in with Rodney two years ago, and gingerly lowered herself onto the edge of what was certain to be more dust mites and dead skin cells than foam and upholstery. "You can't keep doing this."

"I ain't doing nothing."

Precisely the problem.

"How do you intend to live?"

"We're doing just fine."

Clearly. Kate looked away, focusing on the brown film of decades of dirt that obscured the view to the five-by-ten backyard beyond the back door.

"Well..." Mom broached the silence again, her tone pathetically familiar.

As her heart sank, Kate braced herself for the upcoming conversation.

"We'll do fine this month. We'll do better, Katie-bug. I promise we will. I'll take that money and I'll put it in *my* account this time. Rodney can't get to it first that way. And then I'll just go right on down to the lease office and square things with the trailer baron."

"Mom..."

"I will. Just you try me and see, Katie. I'll do it right this time."

How many times could Kate hear the same speech and know the opposite outcome, and yet still give in? Did that make *her* insane?

No. It made her an enabler. This needed to stop. Kate's world was full—overflowing—with chaos. At least this one point, this one thing, she could put to a stop. She turned to fix her gaze on her mother, finding eyes that were shaded the same blue as her own. The face in view seemed oddly unfamiliar though. Mother looked old—much older than her actual years. More than old, she was worn. Or maybe imprisoned. Trapped in a life that either the woman didn't want to leave or saw no hope in escaping, and so had given up.

Kate's heart tugged hard, and not just for her mother. For herself, because she'd seen the same lines tracing in her own skin, the same fading light dim her own eyes. There was nothing quite so demoralizing as feeling like you were trapped.

"Katie-bug, just this one more time—"

"There's no money this time, Mom." The lie coated her tongue with a bitter film. She had a check already made out, waiting in the pocket of her wool coat. This month Kate's royalties had been more than most. It would not only catch up Mom and Rodney on the delinquent bills but get them through the new month as well.

But Kate didn't retract the falsehood.

Mom scowled. "What?"

Stiffening her posture, Kate folded her hands and placed them primly on her knees. "I don't have money to give you."

Mother's lips parted, and she stared for two breaths, then her expression contorted into something ugly. "You selfish girl!"

Kate swallowed but worked to keep her expression stone.

"How many years did I work two jobs for you? Feed you? Gave you this roof over your head?" Her arms flailed upward, and then she rocked forward, closing the foot of the recliner with a hard *thunk.* "How ungrateful can one daughter be? You live in luxury now because of me. And you won't share? Selfish! Selfish! Selfish!"

Kate winced at the burning prick in her eyes. Slowly she lowered her gaze to a stain on the shag carpet near her toes. She could give in. She usually did.

Stop this chaos.

She wanted to stop all the chaos. With her mom. With Jacob. With herself. This was the only one she felt she had the power to do so...

Standing, she forced herself to raise her chin. "I'm sorry, Mother. There's just isn't any money this month. You and Rodney will have to figure out something else—put his disability check to use so that the electricity doesn't get shut off."

The steps back to the entry area were few, but they felt like the hardest of her life. When she bent to replace her boots, she was blindsided by the blow of a musty-smelling pillow. No doubt sent sailing through the air by her mother.

"You're nothing but a gold-diggin' tramp with no gratitude in her heart. God will punish you!"

That seismic rubble moved in Kate's soul again, the burn of pain scalding. Both feet secured in her footwear, she turned her face back to the hateful contours of her mother's. "I'm sorry," she whispered.

A string of expletives followed Kate out the door. But that wasn't the hard rub. What hurt was how much truth there was in Mother's statements.

Kate Murphy had indeed been a gold-digging tramp. And for that, she would be forever trapped.

ThisBoondockingLife entry #28

> *There are so many reasons one might take on this sort of living. The thirst for adventure. A craving for a different life. The drive to discover who you might be…*
>
> *We have our reasons. If you're thinking about this sort of thing, what's yours?*

Chapter Two

(in which the lies catch up)

Jacob stared at the notice in his hand.
Foreclosure.

Reading that word caused a bleak sound in his mind—that like a heavy door closing. The hard *boom* resounded through his imagination. Not the first time. This was his fifth of such letters, four of them for investment properties. Investment properties that had proven a disaster—he was upside down on the loans, and the flips he'd promised Kate would be "easy money" weren't anywhere close to being done. The fifth notice had been for the very place where he was right then—the downtown luxury condo he and Kate called home.

That didn't even account for the notices of repossession he'd opened yesterday. One for his truck and the other for Kate's Land Rover.

His hand quivered, the latest letter condemning him as the ultimate failure rattling between his fingers. As his breath caught hard, his vision blurred and his knees buckled. The Ethan Allen leather sofa broke his tumble to the ground—the furniture being something else he didn't actually own.

All of it was going to go. Every. Last. Thing.

Jacob Murphy stood on the precipice of losing everything, his quest for respect proving catastrophic.

Shutting his eyes and not finding any comfort in the black abyss there, he fought to control his breathing, to regulate the hard, fast hammering of his heart. *It's all going to go. I'll have nothing.*

That thought barely processed before he pictured his wife. *Katie.*

His chest squeezed so hard he would bellow out in excruciating pain if he could draw the air to do so. He couldn't. The agony was like the vice grip of a cruel near-death strangle, and Jacob writhed against the leather beneath him, clutching his head.

Katie...

He'd lose her too. There was no way to stop it.

***

Kate stared at the text Jacob had sent her while she'd been in the trailer with her mother. He wasn't serious, was he?

Thinking you should stay with my parents for the week. It'd do some good.

Her? Stay with Kevin and Helen Murphy for the duration of her visit? Since when had that ever been a thought?

Well, to be honest, there had been a time when she would have taken that idea and embraced it with both arms and her whole heart. There were few things she'd wanted more than to build a good relationship with Helen—and for a time, when they'd first been introduced, it had seemed like a real possibility. Even now, many years after that likelihood had all but withered and died, Kate couldn't deny the longing in her heart to find a friendship with the woman who had become her mother-in-law. The kind of beautiful, loving, mother-daughter type of connection that Kate had witnessed between Helen and the other two—no, now three—daughters-in-law.

That reality pierced Kate's heart deeply. The breach with Helen was a level of rejection she'd never experienced before. Significant, because Kate had been familiar with rejection throughout her life.

Drawing a staying breath, she pushed away the sting of tears and responded to her husband's text.

I'm not sure I'm up for that. In fact, I'm not sure how long I'm going to stay. Might head back home tomorrow actually.

Jacob got her message—she could tell from the *read* notice on her phone. But he took a long time to answer. Certainly he was writing her a lecture on how they (read *she*) needed to try harder. They needed to be the bigger people. To show the Murphy family that she and Jacob were not ashamed and deserved to be treated as legitimate family members, not merely tolerated out of bloodline obligation.

A speech she was not unfamiliar with. One she couldn't necessarily agree with. While Jacob was determined to fight for his place in the world—something that had compelled her to him years ago—she couldn't make the leap to the claim of being *not ashamed.* Nor could she think that this parade of self-sufficient dignity was actually summoning respect from Jacob's parents and brothers. As time went by, in fact, Kate felt keenly that all of her and Jacob's efforts were, in fact, widening the rift.

Jacob refused to see things that way.

Either way, I want you to stay with Dad and Mom.

She pulled back from her phone as she read his directive, feeling her confused scowl pull at her brows. What on earth? Yes, Jacob could be direct, cold even. He usually didn't mean to be sharp—it was simply part of his cut-and-dried personality. But this was not normal. Typically during the trips she made to make sure her mother was not living on the muddied roads of Sugar Creek, Jacob lavished Kate with *Take your time. Enjoy this little break. Stay where you'd like. Eat what you want...* In fact, he was kinder and more generous with her during these trips than he ever was when she was at home, a truth that both confused and angered her.

This change in his attitude was a cold, blindside smack against her heart.

As she lifted her attention from the phone and stared at the rust-stained tin rooflines of the trailers dotting the view beyond her windshield, Kate felt herself shrivel, now smaller than she'd ever been before. Jacob had rescued her from the life she'd just fled, from the quicksand of trailer-park poverty, from the humiliation of being nothing more than white trash. For a time he'd made her feel like a real-life Cinderella, and she was nothing if not grateful.

But seven years of feeling less-than had a way of wearing out the starry-eyed wonder of her very own fairy tale. Jacob never said as much, that she was less-than. But he sure could run over her and make her feel it deeply.

The cheery sound of ringing bells drew her focus back to her phone—the sound of another text.

Thing is, something's off with the credit cards, Katie. I think that it'd be better if you stayed with Mom and Dad—there's no charge for a bed there.

Kate sighed into the softer tone Jacob had used—including the name *Katie*—and the stiff boxing of her heart loosened a bit. Even still, concern ate at her. What could be wrong with the cards?

Should we be concerned? she typed.

No.

Staring at the screen, Kate waited for a better explanation. Jacob apparently thought none was required.

***

Jacob emerged from the shower feeling no less panicked than when he'd stepped under the steaming water. After hours of phone calls and internet chats, seeking legal help for the deep mess he'd plunged into, the only knowledge he'd truly gained was that unless he could catch up payments, those foreclosures would proceed. That, and he was now a ripe target for all sorts of sketchy lawyers and programs that promised to spring him free.

Having called his dad's personal lawyer—a man who helped set up Dad's LLC and went over contracts to make sure Dad wasn't going to be sued if a build unintentionally went south—Jacob had been duly warned *not* to step into any of those predatory traps. They'd only make things worse.

Bankruptcy was the only option Jacob could see. At least that would keep the coming lawsuits at a minimum.

But...*bankruptcy!* Was there a greater antithesis to his quest for success and corresponding respect?

Katie would be so disappointed, adding a deeper wound to Jacob's already gaping shame. After all, she'd married Jacob and not Jackson because Jacob had been the better financial bet. He'd been the surer path out of the generational poverty that had driven her to desperate measures of escape. At the time Jacob hadn't let that injure him too much. He'd gotten the girl, the one who had wholly captured his attention and then heart within weeks of meeting her. That had been all that had mattered to him.

Eventually, he had reasoned, she would come to truly love him. Eventually, when he made all her determined dreams come true, she wouldn't wonder if she'd married the right brother.

Garbage. All of that was pure crap. Especially since Jacob had failed spectacularly.

Bitterness overran Jacob's thoughts, and with it a surge of anger that he desperately needed to release. With only a towel wrapped around his frame, he stormed through the condo, his direction taking him to the office. There, he slammed the door. Kicked the desk chair so hard it sailed across the room and crashed into the wall—breaking the back from the seat and leaving a deep gash in the gray-painted drywall. Still, the rage was not satiated. With one fierce swipe, he cleared the desk. Papers flew up and then rained down, the chaos of it so much of what he felt. His laptop smashed into the shelf beside the desk, shattering the screen and busting the keyboard.

Emotions still roiled hard, but the physical destruction around him caused Jacob to rein in a bit of self-control. As desperate hopelessness engulfed him, he dropped to the floor, the sound of crinkling papers briefly preceding a sound he hadn't heard since he'd been twelve years old.

His own unquenchable sobs.

Clutching his head in his hands, he rocked back and forth as cries that hailed from the deepest hurts and disappointments of his life racked his body.

"God, I'm a loser!"

Nothing in the silent disaster around him contradicted his cry.

***

The early spring sun winked through the evergreen boughs from its lowering position. Kate figured she had about twenty minutes or so before the light would shelter itself behind the mountain on which Sugar Pine stretched, and then the early spring chill would slide into down-right cold—too cold to write anymore.

She drew a breath, sweet with the scent of pine. Against the gentle gurgling of moving water beneath the thin ice covering the creek, Kate stretched and then closed her laptop. She leaned back on the picnic table bench, casting her gaze upward and studying the wispy clouds that drifted against the darkening sky.

The serenity of her setting should have settled her apprehensions—that and having written her angst into her latest work in progress. Unfortunately, both proved only mildly therapeutic. Kate couldn't stop worrying about whatever it was Jacob wasn't telling her, and she fretted over showing up unannounced at her in-law's house to ask for a bed for the night.

The least Jacob could have done was text his mom and let his parents know Kate would come knocking. Perhaps he had—Kate didn't know. Hadn't heard from him again since that last cryptic text hours before.

She blew out a hot breath. *Out, anxiety. Be gone, frustrations. I'm a big girl. I can handle this.* After rubbing her sweater-covered arms and then running a palm over the smooth covering of her computer, she shut her eyes. *Lord, if you have the time to see me, could you make this not be terribly awkward?*

As she flung upward the sincere plea with only a thin hope of it being received, Kate hugged herself. The unrequited tug of her heart moved toward Helen. Kate couldn't help how much she wanted the woman to like her. Not just because she'd married one of Helen's sons, but because Helen was usually a genuinely beautiful soul. Kate longed for acceptance from Jacob's mom. Almost as much as she longed to escape the feeling of being overlooked by God.

If only things hadn't gone as they had seven years before. Truly,

truly Kate hadn't meant for the circumstances between herself, Jacob, and Jackson to take the path they had. It'd gotten so complicated so quickly, and then ugly with even more speed. Was she to forever carry the regret and consequences of mistakes made when she'd been eighteen?

If the status of her relationship with her mother-in-law—not to mention the slippery slope her marriage was on—were any indication, then yes. Yes, Kate would always pay the price.

Lord...

The bells of an incoming call cut short her second shot at a heavenward plea. Sighing, Kate reached for the phone, expecting to see her mother's name on the caller ID. Shockingly, *Helen Murphy* flashed instead.

Kate bit her lip, hope rising even though she told herself not to let it. "Hello?"

"Hi, Kate. It's Helen."

"Yes." Why was Kate so inane when it came to speaking with Helen? She was a wordsmith, after all. Could she really not have a casual conversation with her mother-in-law? She cleared her throat and smiled, hoping a sense of easy confidence would mask the unease in her voice. "Hi, Helen. I was just thinking about texting you."

Helen chuckled. The sound seemed stilted. "How about that? I beat you to it. Kevin just got off a call with Jacob, and he mentioned you might be coming here to stay for a few days this visit."

So Jacob had called. "Uh. Yeah. I mean, if that's okay? It's actually looking like only for the night."

"Just tonight?"

"Yes. I'm thinking I'll head back to Seattle in the morning."

"Your mom being in town is a rare thing, isn't it? And Jacob says you use these trips for work."

Disgrace wrung a hard twist in Kate's chest. The lying thing might be part of the reason Helen and she didn't have the kind of relationship Helen had with Lauren or Mackenzie. Now, probably, with Sadie. Kate's sisters-in-law were not the conniving little schemers Kate was. *Gold-digging tramp.*

Kate pushed against the physical reaction pulsing against her own guilt. "I can work at home. It's basically the same. I just came to see Mom while she was here, and I was able to do that today." Keeping up this manufactured life she'd invented for her mother had long since proven exhausting. Especially when Mom would use it as blackmail—which no doubt would happen again in the near future.

"I see. How is she?"

"Mom?"

"Yes."

"She's..." Oh, to say what was true!

My mom is codependent and lazy. She's also a gambling addict and living with a man who is equal to all her flaws. They've been living off my book royalties—but not actually paying their bills. Today, I cut them off.

What would it be like to confide in someone who wouldn't trash her mom or insist that Kate was a bad daughter for not shoveling out money at her mother's every irresponsible whim? However, Helen, nor any of the rest of the Murphys for that matter, didn't know the reality. Only Jacob knew. And that was solely Kate's fault.

Pride was such a twisted trap.

"She's feeling a bit under the weather, so she's been taking it easy for a while." Heat crawled up Kate's neck as she continued the lie she'd spun years before.

"Oh, I'm sorry to hear she's not well. Can I do anything for her?"

"Oh no." That came out way too fast. "No, thank you. Like I said, I just visited with her today. She had a bit of her...spunk back. No doubt she'll land on her feet and be off conquering the world again in no time."

Yeah. Those feet would be pounding down a path straight to Kate's checkbook. Double time. They wouldn't be off to sign business contracts or to traipse around Europe in lavish style, as Kate had long led the Murphy family to believe.

God, am I really this woman?

No wonder He didn't make the time to answer her prayers. Wretched woman that she was, why would He?

Chapter Three
(in which Jacob exposes the truth)

Jacob stared at his phone, which rested on the coffee table in front of him as if whispering a dare. *Reveal the truth.*

He'd spent years silencing that challenge. The task had been seeded in his soul long ago, and Jacob had done a fine job in gagging it. Now, however, as failure trumped all his pretentious efforts to smother his deep sense of pitiful inadequacy, that directive slithered through his heart and mind unhindered.

Reveal the truth.

To whom?

Who would even care enough to listen to his wretched tales and confessions? No one—and wasn't that the cream of all patheticness? He was one of seven sons born to parents who loved big, the best they could in such a bursting home of varying personalities, needs, and pursuits. How could he claim that there was *no one* in his life with whom he could confide?

There was Dad.

A yearning leapt at that idea. Dad was the measure by which all the Murphy boys judged right and good. Though Jacob knew a few tales of Dad's not-so-squeaky-clean past, to be honest, he had a hard time believing them. Dad was the essence of godly manhood, not to mention a successful entrepreneur and family provider. He was the Paul Bunyan of Murphy lore—obviously bigger than what could possibly be real, but nothing short of inspirational anyway. Jacob could only admire him. By that token, however, he felt incapable of confiding in him. Once done, Jacob didn't think he could handle the depth of Dad's disappointment. He'd never again be able to stand before Dad and not feel like a worm.

As if that wasn't true already.

Though lower than ever he'd been in his life, apparently Jacob wasn't *quite* that desperate. Even still, the whisper toward speaking the truth seeped in his mind.

He reached for the phone and opened the contact list. The first several were for business. His general contractor. The roofer. Plumber. The loan officer. A sour burn churned in his gut. People he owed money. Money he didn't have and wouldn't acquire once the bank foreclosed.

Beneath those, the first name he came to belonged to one who, of his family, reached out to him most often.

Connor.

Connor had always felt a deep sense of responsibility toward everyone he'd ever met. No doubt over the years Connor had called all the Murphy brothers as often as he contacted Jacob. Connor was just that guy. Though likely true, his persistence to reach out to Jacob—the unspoken outcast of the Murphy boys, the least relatable, least likeable of all the brothers—made Connor's diligence something to be marked.

Reveal the truth.

To Connor then.

Before he could reason his way out of it, Jacob hit the Dial icon and slid the phone to his ear.

"Jacob! Good to see your name on my screen." Connor's surprise, though not overdone—because Connor's ways were not like over-the-top-about-everything Jackson's—snagged Jacob's rocking emotions.

"Hey, Connor."

"You okay?"

Connor's immediate concern told Jacob that either (A) Jacob hardly ever called his family, so this phone call signaled a crisis, or (B) Connor could detect the sinking despondency in Jacob's voice. Jacob swallowed against the closing of his throat and wondered yet again how his life had gotten to this dark, dead-end place.

"Jake? Talk to me, buddy. What's going on?"

"I...I just need you to pray for me, okay?" Was it wrong to seek prayer when he'd personally neglected any sort of real relationship with God for years?

"Every day, brother."

Not surprising. Connor was also that guy, the prayer warrior if ever there was one. "Yeah. Thanks."

"Jake, you don't sound good. Do I need to come up there?"

A tear threatened to spill from the corner of Jacob's eye. Fighting it, he squeezed his fist and pressed it against his forehead. "No. I know you can't anyway. Between your job and now Sadie and Reid—no. I just need..." He couldn't finish, and a lengthy pause extended where his explanation failed.

"Talk to me."

Suddenly the soft whisper of *reveal the truth* became an irresistible need to dump out everything. Almost everything.

"Kate and me, we're struggling."

"I kind of figured that a while back. Something happen?"

So much had happened. Was still happening. And the more Jacob tried to stop the disaster, the more he tried to make things work the way he had planned, the way he'd promised Kate, the more everything fell apart.

"We...we've had a couple miscarriages." Why did he start there? That wasn't the crisis he was in the middle of now. Didn't really have any bearing on the mess he was in currently. Did it? Even so, the raw ache of losing something so precious and hoped for—and the loneliness of grieving in silence—pierced. That cut split the dam, and emotion flooded out in unfiltered words. "And we've grown distant. Kate's unhappy. I'm unhappy. And now I'm...I'm in so much trouble, Connor."

"What kind of trouble?"

"I'm about to lose everything. Our home. The cars. My business. It's all in default. Foreclosure. Repossession. Everything is about to go. I can't do anything to stop it."

Silence met his blurted confession, and Jacob could feel

condemnation in it. Why had he said all of that? Any of that? Exposed himself? For what? So he could feel even more like the loser of the bunch?

"Man...Jacob." Connor's soft tone punched down Jacob's rising resentment. "I can figure out a way to get up there. I will."

"No. I don't want you to."

"What can I do?"

"Just...I don't know. I just needed to tell *someone*."

"Someone...does Kate know? I mean, about the foreclosure and things?"

"No. She's in Sugar Pine right now. I can't tell her over the phone."

A sorry excuse. Jacob was a meticulous person. He liked spreadsheets, and making plans, and seeing things work. All reasons that Kate had said she had full confidence in Jacob's ability to make his property speculation successful.

Jacob hadn't been clueless about where everything had been heading the past year. Far from it. Every default notice, every dime he was behind on payments, he knew about all of it. Ignorance hadn't been the problem. He'd just been so desperate to make it all work that he'd convinced himself the gambles he'd taken would pay off. If he could just steel his nerves a little longer, the payday would be worth it.

Turned out, no. No, there would not be a payday. There would by a payout too great for him to ever meet. He was ruined, and he'd taken Kate with him into the depths of insurmountable debt.

Poverty. The place she'd been so desperate to escape that she'd dumped Jackson for him, believing Jacob to be the better bet. Instead, he'd be the one to put her right back in the mire.

"Man, brother." Real empathy carried in Connor's voice. "Whatever I can do, just say the word. Okay?"

Jacob couldn't form words as his chest shuddered in silent cries. "Jake?"

"Yeah. Okay," he choked.

Connor held quietly on the other end, his silence more like

pity than condemnation. Jacob wasn't sure that was much better. Yes, it was. At least he'd not been rejected.

He'd exposed the depth of his failure, and he'd not been castigated as an idiotic loser—though he knew that was exactly what he was. There was something, though small in the weight of all that was bad right then, about not feeling entirely alone.

***

Kate stared at the image on the wall, running a finger along the edge of the barnwood frame. Bobbie Joy's cherub little face stared back at her. Sweet moss-green eyes. A toothless grin. Tiny fists rolled near her ears. Gingered fuzz covering the top of her head in the most adorably wild fashion.

Sorrow split wide in her heart. Bobbie, Kate's niece by Jackson, was nearly six months old. Had Kate carried the last pregnancy to term, her own son or daughter would have been two months older than that.

"She looks so much like Kenzie, don't you think?"

Helen's soft voice startled Kate as the woman eased down the hallway.

"I'm sorry." Helen touched Kate's elbow, the move tentative. "I didn't mean to sneak up on you."

Kate molded a smile, pinning her gaze back on the photo. "She does look like Mackenzie. Though I see Murphy in her too."

"Jackson is bound to spoil her."

"Your boys all have such a soft heart for kids. Must come from growing up with so many siblings."

"Hmm..." Helen slid a half step closer. "Does it hurt to see this little one, Kate?"

Once again caught off guard, Kate looked at Helen. Her mother-in-law winced and then looked at her wringing hands.

"Jacob told me about the baby." When she lifted her face back up, tears shimmed in her eyes. "Did you not know that?"

"No." Her answer came out too sharp. Kate tried again, softer. "No, he didn't tell me."

"I'm sorry. I'm sure he didn't mean to betray you."

Kate felt frozen in exposure. She never knew what to do with vulnerability—especially among people who didn't know the real woman she was. The fragile, lonely version of herself that she kept meticulously hidden behind a veneer of confidence and control. Jacob was the only person in the world Kate had ever allowed past that facade.

But the loneliness of life left Kate with this great yearning. If Helen knew everything—the real story of why she ended up with Jacob, breaking Jackson's heart—would Kate find compassion in the honesty?

At least Kate could try being real with Helen in that moment, even if it meant her emotions slipped from her firm grip a wee bit.

"He didn't betray me." Kate whispered the words around the tightness of her throat. "I just didn't know you knew, but it didn't have to be a secret. We just didn't tell everyone because—" Her voice cracked, control slipping further. "Because it hurt too much."

Helen closed the narrow space between them and slipped an arm around Kate, squeezing her tenderly. "I can only imagine, honey."

As one tear fell, another trailed in its path. Kate quickly wiped them away, uncomfortable with this emotional breach. "It wasn't the first time. We've lost two others."

"Oh, Katie. I'm so sorry."

Katie... Only Jacob called her that. Well, and her mother sometimes. From her mother, she despised the name—it was always manipulation. Hearing it from Helen was like a new beginning. At least there was hope for such.

"Thank you." Kate inhaled a breath meant to regain her self-control and then gave Helen a small smile.

"Was it too hard this past Christmas, with Jackson and Kenzie and Bobbie Joy? Is that why you and Jacob stayed away?"

Kate shrugged. The true answer was yes, that was a reason. Not the only reason, but it was one of them. Attention back on the framed picture on the wall, Kate ran her thumb over the edge of the frame again. "She's precious, and we're happy for Jackson and

Mackenzie. And for you."

She could feel Helen's gaze on her, but she didn't turn to meet it. Though she longed for closeness with this woman, this slide into emotional exposure was becoming too much. Instead, Kate stepped backward, as if taking in the rest of the framed pictures on the wall. Reid Allen, Connor's new four-year-old son, grinned back at her, a fishing pole in his hands.

"Will you have one taken with both Reid and little Bobbie?"

"I sure hope so. I'd love for everyone to get together in May. It seems like too long since this house has been full-to-bursting."

Helen loved nothing more than to have her clan under one roof. Almost everyone else in the family seemed to enjoy it as much as their matriarch. Almost.

"Will Sadie be able to handle that, do you think?"

"I'm praying her treatments are as kind to her as they'd be effective for the cancer."

Kate nodded. If she thought it would make any difference at all, she would pray for her newest sister-in-law the same way. But to Kate, it seemed her prayers were little more than words on the wind. God simply did not have time to hear someone of her insignificance. Or rather, of her ill repute.

Helen moved closer again, once more looping a gentle hold around Kate's shoulders. "I am praying for you too, Katie. Maybe I've never told you that—but I do. I have. I truly want God's best for you and for my son, because I love you both."

That was nearly too much. Kate blinked, and her jaw quivered. Though she was desperate for those words, for that love, she remained a statue. She simply didn't know any other way to be.

Or she was too afraid to be anything else.

ThisBoondockingLife entry #16

> *Romance stories are the best, don't you think?*
> *Obviously I love them (I write them!). Perhaps*
> *you'd like to know mine?*
>
> *Ours was a love-at-first-sight story. But in a*
> *messy way.*
>
> *I wasn't dating Jake when we fell in love. Not*
> *even when we first kissed (scandal!). No,*
> *really, scandal, because this is where it got*
> *messy, straight from the first electrifying*
> *gaze.*
>
> *I was dating his brother—a perfectly nice boy*
> *who really didn't know anything about the*
> *real me at all. Yes, you read that right. I was*
> *dating his brother when I fell in love with*
> *Jake. Years later, that fact still causes*
> *problems.*
>
> *Who says romance is easy?*

Chapter Four
(in which Kate remembers)

Despite Helen's assurances that Kate was welcome to stay longer—the whole week in fact—Kate packed her overnight case, thanked her hostess properly, and pointed her SUV north, setting out for her long drive back. The dichotomy of longing for acceptance and being terrified of disappointment was not lost on her, but she simply could not bring herself to risk more vulnerability.

How could that make any sense? She wanted to be known, but at almost every opportunity she closed herself off. She wanted to be forgiven for things done badly and for hearts having been hurt, but at the occasion to confess and be absolved, she instead fled.

Her life had become a game of hide-and-seek, and she'd become good at hiding. Too good. The shadows, though lonely and cold, were known and less threatening than the light that was sure to expose well beyond the things she was willing to reveal. And then?

Likely, rejection. Likely, more pain. Likely, a whole new depth of loneliness.

This sorrowful burden was her traveling companion as she left her hometown and drove I-5 north. As she passed from one place to the next, familiarity dulled the power of the world beyond her windshield, allowing for the reel of the past to replay unhindered.

She'd been seventeen, almost eighteen, when she'd met Jackson Murphy. Oh, she'd heard of the Murphy clan—anyone at Sugar Pine High would have had their head stuck in an abandoned mine shaft not to have known about the family of seven boys. She'd even seen them at a distance, Jackson in particular, but also his younger brother Tyler, who at the time was the only other high-school-aged boy of the Murphy bunch.

Though not enormously tall, Jackson was built like a lumberjack—word told among the girls at school that all the Murphy guys were muscle heavy because their dad employed them in his small construction business. If looks were true, that situation didn't do the boys any harm and likely had handed Jackson a few favors. Not that he needed them.

Jackson had a head of thick dark hair, and from the distance Kate had usually kept, he owned gleaming brown eyes that lit with laughter. He was pegged as a class clown—his latest prank pulled off shortly before Kate began attending that school. Apparently he'd organized the entire student body to set their phone alarms to go off at exactly 3:29, filling every classroom and hallway with the cacophony of various ringtones one minute before the final bell rang.

The student body thought it was epic. Clever, harmless, and

well played. The perhaps over-tyrannical administration threatened to issue suspension for every student who participated—which had seemed impossible, as that would have been nearly all the students in the school—but Jackson had rushed forward as the perpetrator, and employing his ample amount of charm, had gotten everyone, including himself, off with a *don't do it again*. Also, a few thinly veiled chuckles.

Kate had missed that stunt, but hearing about it sparked her curiosity about this boy who was both eye candy and funny.

Somehow he'd noticed her too. And thought she was something special.

Kate attributed that strange, beautiful twist of luck to her cleverly invented, epic tale about her life. In this fictional version of herself, her mother was a CEO of a multimillion-dollar tech company. The reason Kate hadn't ever been to Sugar Pine High before her senior year was that she'd been schooled via private tutors as she traveled with her mother. But Kate had wanted to experience normal life—a sort of incognito princess type thing. So Mother had allowed her to live with a reclusive aunt in the quiet community of Sugar Pine during the final year of her pre-college education.

It was a much better tale than the one in which she grew up as trailer trash on the wrong side of the creek, in the dumpster community downstream. Her invented backstory gained Kate more, and much better, attention than she'd had previously.

The legitimacy of her tale was never questioned. Why, Kate couldn't explain, as she'd found her designer clothes during painstaking shopping expeditions at thrift stores, never had spending cash with her, and didn't even own a vehicle, let alone drive one. All she had was her closed-off personality and a fictional history.

It was then that she'd discovered she was good with a story. And also then that she discovered that Jackson's family was as wonderful as they were good looking.

Jackson had asked her out. He'd been adorably nervous, and once she'd said yes, he'd paraded her about like she was the princess she'd claimed to have been. It should have made Kate feel victorious. Or at least special. Instead, she felt filthy. Like a rotten poser. And eternally nervous that she'd be found out.

And she had been. But not in the disastrous way she'd feared.

Kate had been dating Jackson for a couple of months by the time his basketball season was nearing its end. Playing the devoted girlfriend that she wanted so very much to be, Kate went to all his home games. She would sit with his mom and dad, and whoever else of the Murphy group who happened to come, and cheer him on quietly. At the last home game, a playoff match, Jackson's older brother Jacob—home from an internship—had attended.

He looked nothing like Jackson. Fairer skinned, lighter hair and eyes, Jacob favored his mother more than any of the Murphy brothers. He also acted nothing like Jackson. Jacob was reserved, perhaps a bit standoffish. More like Kate was herself.

All that had been simple observation. Nothing harmful in that. But there was something about him, a draw that Kate could not define, or deny.

That game had ended in a loss for Jackson's team. A rather ugly one. Disappointment pulsed through the fans, including the Murphys. Kate felt sad for her boyfriend—she knew this wasn't the way Jackson wanted to end his final season of high school basketball.

"It's going to be quite a while before the guys come out of that locker room." Helen stood on the steps to the bleachers, her face tipped toward Kate. "Want to come back to our house with us and wait for Jackson there?"

"No, that's okay. I'll wait here and then head home after I say good night to him. I'm sure my aunt will pick me up." Kate wrangled up her practiced smile.

Truth was, she did this every game, then texted Jackson that she was heading home but had loved watching him play. That way she could catch the late bus heading toward Sugar Creek in the veil of night. A scheme that had worked for weeks.

It seemed it would do so again. She waited the necessary

amount of time for the Murphys to disappear. Then she slipped from the gym into the cold March night, hands tucked deep into her secondhand North Face coat pockets and head bent against the breeze coming off the snow-blanketed hills.

She reached the bus stop with a few minutes to spare and turned her back toward the direction of oncoming traffic, trying to shield herself from the biting wind. When a set of headlights lit her booted feet and then slowed to a stop, she turned, wondering why she hadn't heard the squeak of the brakes and the telltale hiss of the bus.

Because it wasn't the bus.

"Kate." Jacob Murphy leaned across the passenger seat of his car to talk out of the opened window. "It's you, right? Jackson's Kate?" He waited only a moment, during which Kate froze, and then continued. "What are you doing here?"

"I—" She bit her lip.

"Hop in. It's freezing out."

"Uh..."

He popped open the door. "Come on. I'll take you wherever you need to go."

Swallowing, Kate looked down the road, scrambling for a way out of this situation. It wasn't that she was afraid of Jacob Murphy—he seemed a decent guy. Actually, if she was being candid, she'd liked him. Maybe too much.

That was the problem. Not to mention, where would she tell him to take her if she hopped into that car?

"Kate."

Startled, she looked back at him. Connected with those light-blue eyes and then held her breath. Jacob stared at her, lips parting. A sudden warmth rushed her veins, and her heart throbbed.

Next thing she knew, she was buckling into the passenger seat and he was pulling away from the single bench of the bus stop.

He cleared his throat. "So where to?"

"Um." Kate shut her eyes and squeezed her fingers into fists. What had she just done? "Just to the bridge would be fine."

"To the bridge?"

"Yeah, you know. Off the highway, like if you were going to Sugar Creek?" Blast, had she just said that? Heaven help her, she was going to ruin everything just because she was tongue tied about this Murphy boy. The *wrong* Murphy boy.

Jacob drove in silence. When they reached the bridge, he continued across it.

"Just here." Kate spoke too quickly. She exhaled and tried again. "Here is fine."

"Here?" He eased on the brake.

"Yes."

"There's nothing here, Kate." The car stopped, and he turned an intense and questioning look on her.

"There's a trail." Kate pointed toward the trees, lied through her teeth. "Just over there. It goes back to my aunt's. She's a really private person and doesn't like—"

"Kate, there's not a trail over there."

"Yes there is. It's just hidden."

Jacob held her with a look and shook his head. "You get out of this car, and I'll follow you."

"What? Are you a stalker or something?"

His frown deepened, as did the intensity of his eyes. "There's nothing there. I'm not leaving you out here in the cold dark alone."

Kate swallowed hard, frantically searching for a way out of this.

"Tell me where to take you. And it can't be a gas station, a closed business, or some abandoned mine shaft. I'm not leaving you anywhere that has you out in the dark, cold night alone."

She blinked, her lips trembling. Silently, she pointed forward. Jacob pulled back onto the road and guided his car around the curves. For seven excruciating minutes, Kate sat in silence. Everything was over.

Her way out of the life she hated had just collapsed, thanks to this nice man trying to do a good deed. The entrance to Sugar Creek Court loomed on the right.

"Turn here," Kate whispered.

Jacob obeyed without comment.

"This is fine." Her words wobbled.

He scanned the row of dilapidated trailers along the potted dirt road. "Which one is yours?"

Could this get any more humiliating? "Just...never mind. This is good. Please let me out."

"Kate."

"Please." Her voice cracked.

Jacob stopped the car. Happened to be in front of her house, not that she was going to say so, though at that point it obviously didn't matter.

"Thanks." She pulled on the handle that would let her out, and a dim light popped on above the rearview mirror.

"Kate."

This time she couldn't ignore the gentle but commanding way he said her name. Also, she couldn't stop the tears. "Please don't tell Jackson."

"Tell him what?"

She flung her hand toward the trailer home. "Where I live."

"Why doesn't he already know?"

Kate crossed her arms, hugging her middle. "You wouldn't understand."

"No?"

"You already don't understand."

"I don't understand why you would hide where you live from your boyfriend. You're right about that."

"No one knows." She said that too harsh. Too desperate.

"Why?"

"Because I don't want to be the trailer-trash girl for the rest of my life, okay? Just...just swear you won't tell him." She met his eyes, her heart begging so much more than her words could express.

Light-blue eyes met hers, full of concern. Of compassion. His settled look on her felt heavy, but in a warm and strangely beautiful way.

Same way it had the first time he'd kissed her, but that was another memory entirely. One that had happened not long after that night—but before she'd broken up with Jackson. Which made that moment, sadly, more bitter than sweet.

Kate cut memory lane to an abrupt stop. Already upset with her husband for keeping her from whatever was going on, and heart sore from the varied thorns she'd tangled with the previous day, she wasn't up for more painful memories. She'd stop in Oregon, a little more than halfway home, find a hot shower and a soft bed, and turn her thoughts toward the future.

There had to be something better than this.

Chapter Five

(in which Jacob remembers)

The muted sun ebbed a dreary light into Jacob's awareness. Eyes still closed, he rolled onto his side, mindlessly slipping his hand toward Kate's side of the bed. A sleep-hazed habit—one in which he'd trace the length of her blond hair, and, of late, wish that he felt welcomed to also run his fingers along her shoulder. Maybe even gently pull her close until she was tucked up against him. Those last two... Well, it'd been a while since their relationship had permitted that sort of freedom. Lately, he'd only felt the silk of her hair, careful not to disturb her sleep.

That morning, however, he found the pillow vacant and cold. And then the sleepy haze crashed into woke reality.

Kate wasn't there—she was still in Sugar Pine. Likely sleeping soundly in his mom's cozy guest room, snug and warm and blissfully unaware that he'd ruined her life. How was he ever going to tell her?

She'd bet on him, and he'd failed. Spectacularly.

Regret was a raw ache. Sharp and burning and unrelenting. What if he'd never gone back home after that internship eight years before? What if he'd missed Jackson's final high school basketball game? Never wondered why his younger brother's beautiful girlfriend had lied to their parents about waiting for Jackson after the game and, instead, headed alone into the dark and cold night?

He'd have never followed her to the bus stop—at the time only concern propelling him to do such a thing. He never would have discovered her secret. Never would have agreed to keep it from Jackson.

More than anything, he never would have stared into those sorrowful, yearning blue eyes and lost his heart (and quite possibly, his mind) completely.

The night he'd taken her home to the trailer park, Jacob had known. Without a doubt he'd known what had happened in those moments in his parked car sitting in front of Kate's trailer house. Though he was clearly a failure, Jacob had never been a fool.

Except, the path he went down after that moment had all the tracks of a fool. He could have told Jackson the truth about Kate—he'd had no doubt, then or now, that it wouldn't have mattered one bit to Jackson.

But Jacob kept Kate's secret. More, he'd decided to stay home for a time, telling his parents he really wanted to think through the options in front of him for the remainder of the spring. During that time, he'd made it a point to make sure Kate made it home safely.

Because he couldn't stomach the thought of her alone on a bus at night. And because he chose not to be honest with his brother.

He and Kate spent more time together than they should have. He picked her up to take her to school in the mornings, and during the drive from Sugar Creek to the town across the bridge, she shared with him her life. How she'd started working when she was thirteen—legally way too young, but some people didn't care—and how she'd given her earnings to her mom. How her mom had thrown that money, and Kate's hope, away with her lottery and keno addiction.

How Kate felt like trailer trash. And how she desperately wanted a different life. Enough to bring her to lie to an entire student body, including her current boyfriend.

Jacob's heart had filled with compassion for her, which only fueled what he'd felt for her from that first moment of connection.

Two weeks after that first car ride to her house, Jacob stopped short of the trailer park entrance, pulling off the dirt road. He'd discreetly offered her a ride home from some school event she'd gone to. Jackson had to stay—he was part of student council and therefore on cleanup duty. It continued to amaze Jacob how Kate kept Jackson in ignorance, but time after time, she pulled it off. Usually by simply telling him that her aunt was waiting for her at the corner—conveniently out of sight from the school.

How was Jackson that gullible? Jacob couldn't puzzle it, much beyond Jackson's awestruck twitterpation about Kate. Jacob wondered if Jackson wasn't more infatuated with being the guy who snagged the beautiful, wealthy new-girl's attention than with Kate herself. The suspicion was irritating and not too hard to believe since Jackson was a wick when it came to sucking up attention.

So Jacob stepped in to ensure Kate arrived home safely, even knowing he was on a slippery slope.

He needed to come clean about it. And about other things...

Night had cloaked the pines, the creek behind them, and his car in a velvet darkness. Car parked nearly in the ditch, he had turned to look at Kate, heart slamming hard in his chest. "The thing is, Kate, I like you."

Slowly, she tilted her chin so she would meet his gaze. Man, the way she looked at him, all beauty and sweetness and promise. Jacob swallowed, fighting to make his thoughts right. He was doing this to make things right...

"This can't continue." He had to force the words across his throat.

Those blue eyes... He was gone even before she let that one tear slip.

"I know," she whispered.

With his gaze, he followed the trail of that single tear as it trickled down the side of her nose and then found a resting spot just above her mouth. *Don't.* He remembered that thought clearly. He remembered knowing all the consequences. Remembered telling himself one more time that he shouldn't. Even still, he lifted a hand, cupping her jaw, and with his thumb he smudged that droplet across her top lip.

Kate leaned into his hand. "Jake..." His name was a breathy sigh from her lips. His undoing.

He leaned across the space that had already been slim and met her upturned mouth with his. Her lips were soft and moist, the mild hint of salt a reminder of that tear she'd allowed him to see. She yielded to his kiss, her willingness an anesthesia to his warning conscience.

This is wrong. He remembered that thought too—it'd been the reason he'd frozen after only a skimming taste that left him desperate for a full serving.

Kate had stilled too. The slimmest space separated her lips from his. A moment hung between them, one rich with both warning and desire. Her breath fanned his lower lip as her deep-blue eyes whispered a silent plea...

Jacob caved to the longing.

He had no idea how long they made out, only that by the time he put enough space between them to get his head on straight, her hair bore the evidence of his trespassing fingers, the windshield was fogged over, and they were both breathless. Hands trembling, Jacob sought control by gripping the steering wheel. At his side, Kate finger-combed the beautiful mess he'd made of her tresses. What had been heat and want between them slid toward guilt.

"That can't happen again," Jacob said, mostly to himself.

"I know," Kate said.

Keeping his hands firmly locked on the steering wheel, he glanced at her. She sat with her face cast downward. Seeing her clearly weighted by shame cracked his heart.

"Kate, it was my fault. I'm sorry."

She sat stiff and unmoving for a moment, and then her shuddered breath pressed against the silence. "I don't want you to be sorry."

Her confession pulled both relief and confusion into everything that was already messed up inside Jacob about this young woman. She was his brother's girlfriend! But everything in him wanted her for himself. And it seemed like she wanted him...

"What about Jackson?"

Kate looked up again. "Jake..." She was hypnotic, with the way she whispered his name; the way she locked eyes with him, pulling him quickly out of resolve and back toward her. "You see me as I am, and...and...I want you."

What he'd just said couldn't happen again, happened again. And though he stopped and took her home before more lines were crossed, that line had already been crossed.

He was in love with Kate, and Kate was still Jackson's girlfriend.

What kind of brother, kind of man, did that make him?

Jacob closed the door on that closet full of skeletons as he rolled away from Kate's empty place in their bed. Didn't stop the sour burn that oozed into his gut. Once the truth had come out about Jacob and Kate—pathetically weeks after that first kiss and after several more late-night make-out sessions—Jackson had despised Jacob. Rightly so. Jacob hadn't been proud of the way things had gone, and he had been frustrated with both himself for allowing it to continue and with Kate, as she'd put off breaking up with Jackson. She'd had reasons for that, and honestly, Jacob did get it. Sort of.

Jackson though, he'd been livid. And the relationship between Jacob and Jackson, which had already been tenuous for other reasons, all but dissolved. Jacob had become officially the worst brother on the planet.

He'd hated that. Found out that being the despised brother was much worse than being the unnoticed one.

But he'd loved Kate. And finally he didn't have to hide it. She was his.

***

"I'm sorry, ma'am. Your card was declined again. I'm afraid I can't accept it as payment. Do you have another we could try?"

Fire licked her cheeks as Kate took the card the hotel clerk returned to her. She cleared her throat and selected the only other credit card she had—the one she used for her publishing business. As humiliation and disappointment twisted together, she passed the second form of payment across the desk. "This one should work."

The young man tried to smile. It looked more like doubt than grace. "We'll try it."

As the worker ran her business card, Kate wondered what was going on. Was Jacob cutting her off? Had he canceled her card? They hadn't been doing well. Not for a while. Truth be known, from the beginning there'd been struggles. He'd resented that she'd not broken up with Jackson immediately after she and Jacob had first kissed. Now, looking back on that, Kate knew she should have. Her reasons had been flimsy, stupid, and frankly, selfish.

Jackson had been her date to prom, an event that was two weeks after the first time she and Jacob had kissed.

I can't break up with him right before prom, Jacob. That would be so mean.

You don't think it's worse to lie to him?

He's made so many plans. Rented the tux, made dinner reservations, has this whole group thing lined up. He's so excited about it. If I break up with him now, he won't have a date, and it's senior prom, so...

Jacob had glared at her during that conversation, which had been held in his car while parked in the small parking lot of a convenience store. Now, as Kate saw things from a distance, she understood why he'd not been happy with her, and she regretted it. It'd been a dumb thing to do—selfish on her part, as *she'd* wanted to go to her senior prom, and she knew there was no way, under the circumstances, she'd be able to go with Jacob. It'd been mean to Jackson and misleading to Jacob.

Because of that poor decision, the man she'd married less than six months after graduating high school had never stopped doubting her reasons for wanting him. She knew that Jacob forever suspected that she'd chosen him over Jackson because Jacob's future looked more profitable. He could give her a better life immediately. The life she'd already lied to everyone in order to pursue.

She'd never overcome his unvoiced, but very much felt, suspicions.

Things between her and Jacob had deteriorated more and

more, particularly over the past three years while they were dedicating copious amounts of time and energy toward their individual pursuits, each desperate for success. To that, came the heartbreaking devastation of losing one pregnancy after another.

Three miscarried babies.

Jacob had withdrawn from her more with every loss. Made her feel as if she had failed him on her end of the bargain. He'd given her the life she'd clawed for, but she couldn't give him the family he'd wanted in return.

His resentment carved deep.

"That did it." From the other side of the desk, the kid working the registrar slid her Visa across the marbled countertop. "You're set then, Ms. Murphy. One king room for the night."

Kate stared at the card at her fingertip. Her business card. "Thank you."

Not the card to their bank account. *Jacob is cutting me off.*

No. That wasn't it—couldn't be. As cold as Jacob could be, he absolutely had never been a cruel man. Besides, hadn't he told her to stay with his parents because something was off with the cards?

Still. What would she do if he *was* cutting her off? How would she survive on her own?

ThisBoondockingLife entry #14

> *While my husband and I shared an insta-love beginning, Gertrude and I did not. I didn't even know what she was, to be honest. Worse, when she first rolled into sight, I wrinkled my nose. Yep, I really did. Dressed in my $500 mud boots, $900 wool coat, and clutching my $1k purse (I'd been so vainly proud of that ridiculous purchase), I saw that old green bus pull into the diner's parking lot and turned up my nose.*
>
> *I repent now of my ignorant snobbiness. (Repentance has become a consistent theme in my life, but that's not what this entry is about.)*
>
> *Would it help ease your appall at my pretentiousness to know that my disdain was short lived? It was. One step into her adorable gally, and I recanted. Gertrude was my new freedom, and I'm even more grateful for her now than I was on that first fateful day.*

Chapter Six
(in which Kate buys a bus)

Kate didn't sleep well.

Sitting in a corner booth, she wrapped her hand around the warmth of the mug the waitress had just delivered and stared out the rain-streaked window. In the muted light of that dreary morning, she focused on nothing in particular. Cars splashed by, their tires kicking up tails of muddied rainwater. The streetlamps remained lit, highlighting the droplets that entered their glow of weak light, as if doing their best to shine hope. The effort was vain at best. As was hers in trying to banish the sinking feeling of defeat about her life.

Kate shivered and turned her attention back to the table, raising the mug of hot tea to her lips. Her phone lay silently on the table. As silent as it'd been all day yesterday. All the previous night. Not a single text from her husband. No phone call asking how her day had been. When she thought she'd be home.

Not a word.

In the fertile compost of his silence, suspicion had germinated completely. He was done with her. The prize of winning her from his younger, funnier brother had worn away, and she'd become nothing more than a burden to him.

Shutting her eyes, Kate wanted desperately to pluck the accusations against her husband that were sprouting in her mind. They wouldn't budge, and under the blackness of their ugly proclamation, she felt her heart hardening.

"Your toast, miss." A clatter of plate against table quickly followed the server's announcement.

Kate looked up, steeling against the heat that threatened to climb up her neck and into her face. "Thanks."

"Anything else?"

"No, thank you."

The waitress pursed her mouth in a frown. "Okay."

Not the type of order that would command a decent tip. Kate understood, but she wasn't even hungry for the toast, let alone a full breakfast. The slim woman who scooted back toward the kitchen didn't need to worry. Kate would leave her a healthy tip either way. She always did.

The rumbling of an engine garnered her attention, along with the squeak of brakes sounding just beyond the window at her side. Mindlessly, she turned to look. A green bus pulled along the far side of the diner's parking lot. At least, it was shaped like an old bus. Didn't have the markings of a bus though.

What was that thing?

Through the side window of the vehicle, Kate saw the driver swivel and then stand. Then he stooped, picked something up, and placed it in the window.

For Sale.

Kate inhaled, her immediate interest a shock. Why would she care if an old green bus was for sale? Who would want an old bus anyway? What would one do with such a thing?

Live in it.

She wanted to laugh out loud. *Live* in an old bus? This, from a woman who had become a shameless liar in order to get out of trailer-park living?

If moving into a bus was anything, it was moving down in the world.

The man from the bus stepped around the nose of the thing, flipped up his collar on his denim jacket, snugged his ball cap over his face, and jogged toward the diner entrance. The small bell over the door tinkled a cheery announcement as he stepped through the door, and he strode to the bar counter.

"How's the morning, Sam?" he called toward the kitchen.

"Wet." The gruff response came from some unknown source behind the counter. By the deep tone, the owner was a man. "Any luck with the skoolie?"

What the heck was a skoolie?

"Not yet."

"Shocker. That old beast is a sight."

"Don't say mean things about Gertrude."

Gertrude? Was that the name of his green machine or his girl? Watching as if sucked into a miniseries, Kate sipped her tea and nibbled on her toast, waiting for the next scene to play out. Soon enough, a burly man wearing an apron appeared from the back kitchen.

"Not mean, son. Thing is, you're a special sort of unique. Gonna take a lot of luck to find another nut who wants your remodeled bus-home. Most people prefer their house without wheels."

Amen to that. Except...

Kate lowered her chin and slipped her look from the men at the counter to the green bus parked outside.

Gertrude then. Hmm...

What was she even thinking? Did she really want to return to trailer-park life?

Wouldn't have to. She could travel. She'd always wanted to see the national parks. And freedom—hadn't she craved freedom? More than the security of money, she'd wanted the freedom of having the funds to do whatever she wanted. Maybe it hadn't been funds she'd needed after all. Just wheels...

What about Jacob?

Kate returned her gaze to the table in front of her, finding her silent phone still there. Within her purse at her side, there was a now-useless bank card. An icy jab sliced through her chest.

Jacob *was* cutting her off.

Yesterday she'd taken control of the chaos between her and her mother. It'd been hard, but she'd done it, and it felt good to not be a slave to Mother's demands. It felt empowering to own her own path. Maybe now was the time to get a grip on other parts of her life. Specifically, her disintegrating marriage that, once completely crumbled, would leave her alone and homeless.

No. that was not going to happen. She was a clever woman who could think for herself. Stand up for herself.

She'd needed to figure out what to do, even with her heart aching at her husband's cold rejection. Rather than wilting under that pain, she'd use it for fuel. She just needed a plan.

Maybe Gertrude was the plan. It was shelter. Freedom. And right there for the taking.

Apparently God enjoyed irony.

After casting one more glance to that green machine—and hey, it really wasn't ugly. Not at all—Gertrude was rather cute, in an old, repurposed, bus-ish sort of way. The way that was adventure and a fresh dose of new direction. After that glance, Kate brushed the toast crumbs from her fingers, determining that now, when the cook had sauntered his way back into the kitchen and the ball-capped bus owner was sipping his freshly poured coffee, was as a good a time as any to dig deep and find her old bold self.

She'd reinvented herself once before. Certainly she could do it again.

Clutching her still grave-silent phone and her purse, Kate stood and pushed her shoulders straight. With strides that felt more confident than she actually was, Kate aimed her direction at that Gert-bus owner.

"Excuse me?" Stopping a few feet from his elbow, Kate leaned against the bar-height counter and tapped her nails on the metal back of the stool.

Denim and ball cap turned and looked at her. "Yeah?"

"That's your bus?"

A slow, easy grin spread on his lips. "For the moment. She's for sale."

"I heard."

"Interested?"

"Maybe. Why are you selling?"

"Well, you see, I changed old Gert from a run-down yellow piece of rusted death I bought at auction into that green beauty you see out there."

"I gathered that."

"Then I met this woman..."

Ha. The perennial plot. There was always a woman involved in this sort of story. The sad demise of a man's hopes and dreams... She imagined how Jacob would someday tell his sad tale: *I was coming home for a visit, a welcomed brother among seven. Then I met this woman...*

And she'd ruined his life. Destroyed his relationship with his family. Drove him to become a workaholic. Left him childless. And bitter.

Kate pushed away those thoughts, telling the storyteller within to hush for just a few blessed moments, thank you very much.

"My Sally loved Gertrude as much as I did. We saw amazing things in that traveling home of ours. Spent two years out there going wherever the road would take us. But alas, Sally's grandmother passed, and she left Sally her small acreage along with a run-down little shack. That's our new adventure, and it's gonna be a good one. Also, I'm gonna be a daddy."

His smile grew to beaming proportions. Thrilled, that was what he was, and it twisted the knife already embedded in Kate's soul. The first time she'd told Jacob they were expecting, he'd had the same sort of look.

The man shook his head. "But I can't let Gertrude sit. She wasn't meant for the idle life, only to return to a rusted shell of lost potential."

This guy was poetic.

Despite Kate's horrible week and the bitter ache throbbing through her veins for the past few days, she pushed away the sadness of her life and smiled. He had a way about him, that was for sure. An easy kindness that made her want to become something similar.

"How did you pay for gas and food and things while you were traveling?"

He shrugged. "Did odd jobs here and there. Helped with some fruit harvests. Shoveled snow. Cleaned gutters. Worked a couple summers at national parks. Did a couple of runs of sugar beet harvest. There are lots of things to do, you know?"

No, she didn't know, but that was interesting. "Was it enough?"

"Money?"

"Yeah."

"Sure." He sat back and gave Kate a good once-over. "Thing is, life doesn't require all the fancies." His gaze snagged on her purse, and she wondered if he was guessing how much she'd spent on it.

Way too ridiculously much. That was how much.

His eyes found hers and held. "We did just fine on about seven hundred dollars a month, most months. If we weren't traveling far. Rice and beans. Locally grown seconds produce—you know, the fruits and veggies that are fine but don't look pretty enough for a retail store? They sell pretty cheap..."

"What about hook-up costs?"

"Didn't usually pay them. Gert's fitted with solar power and heated with a small wood-burning stove. Works good for cooking too, once you learn how it's done. A dutch oven became our most valued tool."

Kate nodded.

"Interested?"

Was she? She looked over her shoulder and through the rain-splattered window. The green monstrosity looked a whole lot less like an eyesore and more like charming freedom than it had when it'd first pulled in.

She could see places she'd only ever read about. Take to the open road, her shoulders no longer strapped with a heavy weight of guilt and the ongoing, exhausting need to pretend things that simply weren't so. And she could write. It could be a good life—a much better life than the one to which she was currently shackled.

"Can I look inside?" Kate turned back to him.

He was already off his chair, tugging on his hat, as if he'd known what she would say. "You bet." With a hand, he motioned for the door. "Sam, keep that bacon warm. I'm showing Gert."

Sam poked his head around the window. "Don't let him talk you into anything crazy."

A moment of hesitation held Kate near the counter. "Is he going to rob me blind?"

"Nah. Bryce is a good one. A bit of a nut, if you ask me. But a good one. Biggest heart of gold you've ever seen." He shook his spatula at the man now holding the diner door open. "Don't you try to talk her into anything though. Not everyone thinks that the bus life is the way to go."

"Of course not. I wouldn't let Gert go to just anyone, anyway."

Kate took in the man's expression, and she believed him.

Following him through the rain required that she jog, and once again she was glad she was wearing the plaid mud boots she'd worn to her mother's, even if right then she felt a bit ashamed at the amount of money she'd paid for them. This guy could have lived for nearly a whole month with the cash she'd spent on her footwear. And he'd been happier than she'd been while doing it.

They reached the side of the bus that faced away from the

diner, and he pushed open the door. Kate followed him up the
steep stairs. The risers had been covered in light-colored wood
planks that had lines carved in them for grip, she supposed.

"Well, here we are. My old home on the road." He looked
down the galley way, a sad sort of love in his eyes. "It's been good
to me. To both me and my wife." With that, he stepped back
until he was nearly plastered against the windshield and motioned
for Kate to go ahead of him.

She climbed the last step and slid around him. The floor was
covered in wide wood planks, the same that had been on the steps.
Directly behind the driver's seat was a butcher-block counter and
a deep, though small, stainless-steel sink. The cabinets, all below
the counter, were a hodgepodge of likely whatever he could find
that would fit. He'd sanded them down and whitewashed them.
Across from the small kitchen area was that small woodstove he
mentioned, and an anchored bus seat turned so that the back was
flush with the wall. It was covered in what looked like soft white
wool of some sort and had a gray pillow embroidered with *home*
in green. Directly behind that was a lofted double bed. Another
eclectic collection of drawers and cabinets filled the space between
the floor and the bed, all whitewashed as well.

"That skinny drawer there"—the man came behind her,
pointing at a long, slim drawer directly beneath the bed—"it's a
table. You just slide it open, and a leg drops down. Big enough for
two."

"Clever." Kate inhaled, taking in the scents of linseed oil, worn
leather, burned wood, and the lingering hint of bus that had
managed to survive its dual lives. For some reason, that made her
smile. "It's charming, Mr...."

"Miller. Bryce Miller. And my wife is Sally—I think I told you
that."

"Yes. It's nice to meet you." She glanced around again. There
was no disguising this was a school bus. But it was the most
charming school bus she'd ever seen. "What do you call this
again?"

"Gertrude?"

"No. I mean, yes. I got that part, but—"

"Oh!" He clapped his hands. "It's a skoolie. This one's made from a 1951 Ford F-5. Rescued her out of an auction yard in Arizona."

His enthusiasm made her chuckle. "I'm not sure you're ready to part with this."

Bryce looked around, affection in his gaze. "It sure was fun. Every part of it, from finding this thing, to making her shine, to living the way we did." His attention fell back on Kate. "But it's good to know when it's time to let go. Time to try something new. You know? It's time for me and Sally. Maybe it's time for you?"

Kate took in the miniature living arrangement around her. Yes. Maybe it was that time. "How much are you asking?"

Bryce named a price that Kate thought was low for the work and condition this interesting little contraption was in. Mentally, she ran through her accounts—the money she had saved for business, for the stubborn hope that when a baby came, she'd be able to surprise Jacob with a Kate-funded shopping spree that would make him proud of her, and for the inevitable times every month her mother would call needing funds. With what she *hadn't* given to her mom this month, Kate had enough. Just barely, but enough.

She looked over the small space again, imagining herself tucked up on that bed, typing away at a new story. Maybe glancing up now and then to look out of the rectangular back window at El Capitan, or perhaps to gaze over the Grand Canyon. Maybe she'd be in the Arches National Park. Or maybe even all the way up at Denali. The possibilities sent a thrilling ripple through her veins.

"If I give you a check, will you hold it for me?" Kate turned to look back at Bryce, who leaned, cross-armed, against the giant steering wheel.

"Sure, I can do that. How long do you think you'll need?"

"I need to get back up to Seattle—that's where I live right now—and get a few things settled. Shouldn't take more than a week, I think." The thrill of leaping into something new and daring eased a bit, making room again for the sadness of her life.

Kate hardened against it. There had to be more to life than what she and Jacob had shared so far. Undoubtedly, her husband would agree.

Jacob would likely thank her. Well, no, he wouldn't. But he'd be relieved to be done with this long, drawn-out rescue mission gone wrong. He'd be free to make his life into something he actually liked. Maybe even find his place with his family again, having things less complicated by her absence.

And Kate would have Gertrude as a shelter, the road as an escape, and long quiet nights in which to grieve unhindered.

"A week it is." Bryce stepped toward her, hand stretched out.

Kate met his palm with hers, and they shook on it. "It's a deal."

She would always love Jacob, and never having gained his true affection would forever be the deepest disappointment of her life. But at least on her own, perhaps she would have a chance to heal.

Someday her life would get better.

Chapter Seven

(in which honesty is painful)

Jacob froze when he heard the click of the front door.

He was in his sweats, sitting on the floor in the middle of the office, papers strewn in every direction around him, his older laptop—the one he hadn't destroyed in a fit—open with a jam-packed spreadsheet on the screen. At the sound of footfalls against the travertine-tiled entry, his heart pounded.

Kate was back.

She shouldn't have been home for three more days. That had been the plan. She was going to finish her visit to Sugar Pine, staying at his parents' home, and then come back as scheduled. Giving him a chance to figure out this mess.

"Jacob?"

Concern—maybe it was confusion?—etched her voice.

Jacob pinched his eyes shut as he envisioned the front room. Last he'd been out there, it'd been a disaster. First thing that morning, he'd had a phone call from his general contractor wondering why the electricity had been cut off from one of the project sites. Yet another issue he didn't know how to circumvent. Once again, the gravity of Jacob's situation had crushed him.

In a fit of fury and desperate frustration, he'd defaulted to another temper fit. Throw pillows had sailed through the air. Chairs had been kicked across the gleaming dark wood floors. The credenza had been cleared with a hard sweep of his arm. The floor became littered with broken pieces of lamp and papers, toppled chairs, and dislodged pieces of sofa. None of it had made him feel any better, and he'd escaped to the office without picking up any of the evidence of his loss of self-control. Once in the office, he'd pulled out files and papers and with frantic energy, and he'd begun going through everything all over again.

There had to be a way out of this. He just needed to think harder. Find a way to be clever, to outrun this disaster...

"Jacob?" Now Kate's tone was sharp and drawing nearer.

Jacob slapped the laptop shut and crammed his hand through his hair. *Think!* Kate would be hugely disappointed in him. She'd think he was a failure and regret giving up Jackson for him. He'd lose the last thin thread of connection that had kept her with him.

To everyone he loved, he'd be a failure. How ironic was that? He'd worked like an insane man to look like the success he'd wanted everyone to think he was. Took risks that he'd known were knocking on the door of the outrageously foolish, telling himself the bigger the gamble, the better the payout.

Idiot! How could he have done this?

"What's going on, Jacob?"

He couldn't bring himself to look at her. Instead he squeezed his eyes shut, imagining the look of condemnation he felt sure she held on him.

"Have we been robbed?" Kate stepped into the office—he could hear her slide papers out of her path as she picked her way toward him. "Goodness this is a mess..."

Pulling in a breath, Jacob tried to straighten his spine before he looked at her. *Man up, loser.*

He couldn't. Instead, with both hands, he cradled his head. Seven years of trying to prove she'd chosen the right brother. Years of working beyond realistic capacity to prove himself worthy of respect and notice. Years of never being good enough...

Seven years of failing, leading to this ultimate, cataclysmic disaster.

The weight of it collapsed on him, and he folded.

"Jake!" In two steps, defined by the crush of papers, Kate was kneeling at his side, hands gipping his shoulders. "What's wrong?"

"It's over, Kate."

With a sharp inhale, she stiffened and drew back. Jacob dared a peek at her, finding her expression hard, her eyes cold.

"What?"

Had he hoped he'd find compassion in her reaction? Her total lack felt like a spike driven deep into his back, cruelly piercing his heart. Where he'd just been grieving, anger filled to overflowing. Where he'd felt the drainage of self-respect, now was the surge of fierce self-defense.

"Your sugar daddy is no more." He sat up and glared at her. "I lost it all, Kathrine. Everything. Within thirty days, everything we have will be repossessed, auctioned away, and we will be penniless. Do you want to know why?" He didn't really care whether she wanted to or not. "Here's why. I can't meet your expectations. I can't make the standard you have set. Endlessly trying has driven me to stupid measures, and I gambled everything in a desperate attempt to satisfy you!"

"What?" The word was an exhale, as if he'd just landed a fist in her middle. Kate sat back, first on her heels and then on her backside, and stared at him with a mixture of incredulous pain that Jacob would not have imagined from her. Disdain, yes. But not this expression of woundedness.

Not anytime recently, anyway. Tears sheened her eyes, but she refused to let even one drop fall. Kate was a tough woman like that. Used to be he'd admired that about her. Now...

Now he didn't know.

He didn't know anything anymore. By her stunned silent reaction—not the clipped response and quick exit he'd expected from her—Jacob didn't know his wife anymore.

"Jake..." Her voice cracked on the use of the name anyone rarely used with him, and then her lips pinned together. But she stayed. Her head bowed, arms wrapped around her knees, Kate remained with him rather than storming out.

Jacob drew in a breath he hoped would steady him and looked at the disaster about them. *It's my fault. It's all my doing...*

"I'm sorry," he choked.

Another quick breath, and then her gaze was back on him. Shocked.

Jacob pushed his words forward. "What I just said wasn't...right. Fair. I made bad decisions..."

"What's going on?" Kate fingered a loose tress of her light hair, tucking it away from her face. "Please tell me what you're talking about."

Once again he shut his eyes and braced himself for the confession. "I took on too much debt, too many properties. With the recession..." He paused, shook his head, and stared at the fibers in the rug beneath his feet. "I haven't made payments in months. Notices have been served. Foreclosures. Repossessions." With the last of his failing courage, he met her blue eyes one last time. "I've lost everything."

It was, perhaps, the most honest he'd been with his wife. Ever.

He'd never felt so fearfully exposed.

***

Kate remembered the day she found out her mother had spent everything they'd saved on lottery tickets. Specifically, she remembered how deeply that betrayal had sunk, how intensely it had cut.

Sitting on the littered office floor with her broken husband, she remembered all of it with a visceral clarity, because this feeling was the same. Part of her wanted to scream. To pick up the papers and throw them, to roll her fists and beat them against her husband's chest. How could he have done this—specifically, how could he have *not said a thing* to her about it before?

Life had forever been out of her control. It wasn't fair. Why could she never take the wheel, steer her own trajectory where she wanted to go? Make a plan and see it through. Worse, why were the people she'd entrusted her heart and hopes to continually leading her into disaster?

She was so blind.

She pressed her fingers to her eyes, her mind whirling.

"Kate..." Her name was a sob on Jacob's breath. "I'm so sorry."

"You're sorry?" she seethed on a whisper. She glared at him. "You're sorry? How long have you known this was coming?"

He looked at his closed laptop. Answer enough.

"Why didn't you tell me?"

His jaw worked hard, and he rubbed his neck. "I didn't know how—didn't want you to worry."

"No." Kate leaned closer. "I can't believe that. You didn't want me to know. That's all. No one ever wants me to know, because if I'm kept ignorant, I'll just go along with everything like a blind fool. Just as I've always done."

Wincing, Jacob shook his head.

"I'm done with it, Jacob. I'm done being tossed around by every stupid whim. People I've trusted. People I've—" Hard emotion cut the words short. She pushed it down and pulled up a harsh, resolved tone instead. "I'm done living in the dark, being kept blind."

Shoulders rounded and low, Jacob remained painfully silent.

"Do you hear me?" Kate grabbed the nearest paper, balled it up tight, and fired it at his head. "I'm done!"

He inhaled a shuddering breath, and his shoulders quivered. "I hear you," he whispered.

Kate had never witnessed Jacob with zero fight. If he was anything, he was ridiculously stubborn, followed closely with resolutely defensive. Never was he...

Beaten.

He looked at her, the movement seeming forced, and yes, there was broken agony in his eyes. "What will you do?" he asked, so soft she nearly couldn't understand.

So strange. In that moment when she had everything she needed to get up and get out, something seeming almost divine whispered to her soul that here, in this place, there was...providence.

Kate wasn't sure she could trust that. Didn't even really know if she believed in *providence*. Even so, a curl of pity wrapped her heart, soothing the anger that had just burst forth. She had a plan—the skoolie—and she could rub it in his face, proving to him that she wasn't the wispy fool everyone took her for. *He* took her for.

But that look in her husband's eyes, and that whisper deep in her heart...

It hurt. She hurt, and not just for herself. That pain in her chest was for him. Swallowing, Kate fingered the stubborn lock of hair that kept sliding over her face, once again anchoring it behind her ear.

"I need to think," she said hoarsely.

Jacob nodded.

"Can I stay...tonight, I mean?"

The last of his tenuous self-control crumbled before her eyes, and tears rolled down his cheeks. "I've never asked, and I would never ask, you to leave."

Nodding, Kate stood and turned to exit the office. At the door, her name on his breath gave her pause. She kept her back to him though.

Jacob's voice came heavy. "I wanted to give you everything."

Kate didn't need to turn to know his eyes were on her—she felt them. A collision of anger and heartbreak, betrayal and compassion stormed within. She stepped from the office, away from Jacob. She was glad she'd bought the skoolie, but she wasn't sure she could actually leave him. Not when he'd sounded so sincerely heartbroken.

Not when she was too.

***

Jacob had no idea how long he sat there. His legs had gone numb, and he'd long since missed supper by the time he raised himself off the carpet. Doing so took real effort—like he was eighty-eight, not nearly twenty-eight.

Though he thought he'd tried, he hadn't fully imagined the depth of despair he felt when Kate pronounced their end. It had been the hard stop to his terrifying fall. The shattering of everything he was. Losing everything else combined hadn't been as agonizing as hearing her say she was done. They were done.

Shadows drew long lines against the floor as he made his way into the front area of the condo. The large west-facing windows directed the early evening shadows toward the north and east walls, spilling weak, lackluster light against the kitchen cabinets and the small, modern French-style pedestal table centered beneath a three-tiered platinum-and-crystal chandelier. A soft roll of thunder rumbled beyond the dark-paned windows.

The mess he'd made earlier that morning remained. Jacob moved with uninspired energy, picking up cushions and replacing them on the sofa, re-shelving books, sweeping glass and dumping the shards into the garbage.

If only his life could be fixed with so little effort.

A sniff behind him led him to pivot and face the woman he'd let down and lost.

Kate's eyes were red rimmed and her cheeks puffy. It wasn't often his wife let her emotions roll, and seeing her broken and vulnerable made his own eyes burn yet again.

She smoothed her expression into a more familiar perfectly-in-control look. "I think we should be honest."

Confusion tugged against the tattered corners of his mind. He'd laid everything out to her. Still, he dipped a slight nod. "Okay."

Wrapping her arms around herself, she spun to face the windows, giving him only a profile of her face. "I don't know that we could ever last together. Even without the bankruptcy. You and I...we were wrong from the beginning."

He thought the pain couldn't get worse after she'd declared their finish. He'd been wrong. Breathing felt impossible for the grip fisting him. "Kate, I don't think—"

"Let's not lie anymore." She turned to pierce him with a demanding look. "You wanted me because that way Jackson couldn't have me. You saw me as a way to get back at your brother for always overshadowing you."

Jacob's lips parted, and a rush of air spilled from his lungs. If she had kicked him in the gut, he couldn't have felt worse. As the ache washed through him, anger traveled its wake. "Is that what you think?" he began with a low tone. "Is that what you've always thought?" He lifted his shoulders straight, stepping toward her. "I am nothing more than a lowly thief, thinking only of injuring my brother? Thank you, Kate. Thank you for playing the game with me so well. What do I owe for your services?"

"Don't act like it isn't true, Jacob."

"Me, the actor? How about we try some truth on you, shall we? Why did you choose me over him, Kathrine?" He crossed his arms and inched nearer until he towered over her stubborn upturned face. "Hmm?"

She winced as a dark flush reddened her cheeks, but she did not answer.

"Come on now—say it. You've pinned me with ulterior motives. Now own yours. You thought I was the safer bet. Your ticket out of the poverty you despised. It wasn't *me* you wanted. I was never anything more than a game of roulette to you, and you're only angry now because the house won."

Suddenly tears washed from her eyes. For a moment, Jacob thought sure she'd slap him. Instead she hid behind her hands and sobbed. The harshness of his words echoed in his mind, pummeling him again with what a failure he was.

Jacob crammed his fingers into his hair and held his head. "Kate..."

She continued to cry. With a tentative reach, he touched her elbow.

"Did you ever love me?" she whispered.

With all his very messed-up heart, he'd loved her from the beginning. Didn't she know that was the *only* reason he'd done what he'd done to his brother?

Clearly no, she didn't know. And right then, standing there ruined with her, he doubted she'd believe anything he said. They were both too emotionally strung out to think clearly, let alone discuss anything. The last thing he wanted was a third go-round of destruction.

She hadn't retreated from his barely there touch, so he wrapped a gentle hold on her arm. When she didn't bolt away, he gently tugged her close. He slipped an arm around her shoulders, and she shocked him by leaning her head against his chest.

Thunder rolled through the darkening sky outside, and Jacob felt the storm building.

"God, help," he whispered.

And he hung on to Kate.

ThisBoondockingLife entry #31

> *There is something truly breathtaking after a storm. I'm not talking just any storm, mind you. I'm talking the fiercest of storms. The kind that rocks the skoolie, making you believe it might just overturn. The kind that possesses the sort of thunder that jars your soul. Rain pelts like steel against the metal roof. Lightning gives you a clear understanding of what real power is—and that it does not belong to you.*
>
> *But then...*
>
> *The fury drains. The energy dies. The thick darkness of storm clouds clears away.*
>
> *There is a newness. Everything drips, freshly cleansed. Even the air smells of life and hope.*
>
> *It's as though all things have been made new. The paradox is astounding.*

Chapter Eight
(in which plans change)

The argument in Kate's mind continued.

Curled up alone in the king-sized bed—as she had all night, because Jacob slept on the couch—she peered into the gray dimness of the barely dawn hour.

Last night she'd gone out to tell him that she'd bought the skoolie and was leaving in the morning. Somehow that little bit of honesty hadn't made it to her tongue as she'd intended, and instead she'd flung horrible accusations at him.

Because for years, she'd believed them to be true—and in that awful moment, the allegations refused to be tamed. Jacob's return volley of charges had pierced deeply, but into that wound he'd also brought that silent touch, his fingers on her arm, hand to her shoulder. Finally, arms pulling her nearer. Holding her.

It'd been a long time. So, so long since they'd shared any sort of meaningful connection that even though it had happened in the midst of an ugly, bloody battle, his touch shook the foundations of her doubts about him. About them.

And oh, how she'd longed to be held.

Even with seven years of thinking she'd been merely the prize he'd claimed from the brother he'd resented, Kate still yearned for Jacob's heart. She still clung to the scattered moments throughout their time together when it seemed that Jacob's affection had been involved. For all the reasons she had to doubt it, she still wanted it to be true.

She still wanted him to love her. Did that make her pathetically desperate?

The light scattering the gray of lingering night strengthened, hinting that for the first time in three days, she might see a blue sky. Finger-combing her hair, then twisting it over her shoulder, Kate placed her bare feet against the luxuriously soft shag rug and rolled her toes into the plush warmth.

With two steps, she was able to pull back the drapes, allowing the morning sun more than a sliver's touch into the room. Brilliant white-yellow light dumped into the space, completely smothering the dreariness that had lingered. Kate felt the warmth, tipped her chin upward to receive the light, and let her heart settle into that moment of peace.

Into the rare quietness of her mind, a gentle prodding whispered.

Build a bridge.

To Jacob? Kate wasn't sure how. Or even if she could—more, if she did, if it would matter. They were both so disillusioned. So bitter.

A canyon existed between them. How could she bridge that?

To her question, a series of images surfaced. First of her

husband, sitting in the middle of a disaster in the office, head in hands, entirely broken. And then of her new acquisition, the skoolie. Last, her mind summoned the face of the man she'd purchased it from. Bryce Miller seemed all joy and enthusiasm and peace. He and his wife had lived in a bus, and he was clearly a happier person than either she or Jacob had ever been, though they had lived in the trappings of wealth and luxury.

Kate was willing to try a different life, even if it seemed on the surface to closely resemble what she'd been desperate to leave behind. Would Jacob?

With all the stormy gaps between them, was she brave enough to ask?

She gazed at the inspiring sunrise as light made the tops of the cityscape gleam gold and silver. She and Jacob were about as broken as a couple could be, not to mention financially ruined. Did they have anything more to lose?

Ignoring the hissing worry that, yes, she stood to lose more, that there could well be more pain if she did this—made this offer, rather than making the clean break she'd planned—Kate strode from the room.

Jacob leaned back against the sofa, his face tipped up, eyes closed, expression strained. Kate wondered if he'd slept.

"Jacob?" she whispered.

He straightened, tortured eyes finding hers.

"Did you sleep at all?"

"Not much." Clearing his throat, he sat forward. "Kate, I can't think a way out of this, but—"

"I did something a couple of days ago."

His mouth snapped shut, and a fresh wave of fear passed through his gaze.

Kate sat on the edge of the nearest chair, her hands lost in the long sleeves of her oversized shirt. "I bought a...a skoolie."

"A what?"

"A bus."

"You bought a bus?"

"A skoolie. It's a bus that's been converted. To live in."

His eyes widened, and then he blinked. "You bought a bus to *live* in?"

Kate pressed her lips together and then nodded. In his silent stare, she imagined his thoughts. Why would she do that—to leave him? The answer to that had been yes, and a burning flame crawled up her neck, even though she had a list of reasons to do exactly that.

Jacob turned his attention toward his hands, which he balled together. "How did you pay for it?"

"The royalties from my books. I've been saving..." Kate swallowed, feeling like a teenager who'd been caught in a web of lies.

His gaze flew back to her. "Your royalties? I thought you gave that money to your mom."

"Some of it, I usually do. Not this month though." The heat spread, creeping over her face. There lay another mess neither of them had dealt with well.

"But...I mean, how much do you make?"

"Not a ton. Some months are better than others. But as I said, I've been saving."

"Saving..." His voice held distant accusation, and again she suspected his thoughts. Instead of launching into what felt like the makings of another fight, Jacob slumped back, ran a hand through his thick hair, and then looked at her flatly. "At least you've got something. I'm glad for you." By his tone, all the fight had died in him. He'd resigned to losing everything, including their marriage.

Jacob Murphy sat before her a man defeated, a sight she'd never dreamed she'd witness. And it broke her heart more than she would have guessed. Kate couldn't look at him for the ache of it.

"You could come with me," she whispered.

She heard the movement of his head against the cushions, felt the weight of his stare in the silent moments that throbbed between them. Finally, through a voice as tight as a wire about to snap, he said, "Do you want me to?"

Kate forced herself to see him. Truthfully, she didn't know

what she wanted. When she met his blue eyes, finding them sheened and troubled, she flinched. There was still so much hard space between them—a bridge seemed impossible. Trying might be foolish.

Still, she nodded.

***

Jacob's heart throbbed into the silence. He sat stunned, humiliated, and yet...yet with a feeling so deep for this enigma of a woman that he thought he might drown in the painful mystery of it.

She'd bought a skoolie...to live in? That had every mark of desperation—and that surely had been fueled by her resentment of him. Her intent to somehow leave him.

Why would she offer him this?

He studied her while he tried to make sense of what had just been held out to him. The morning sun touched the crown of her head, making her hair a white-yellow gleam with a hint of warm apricot. Though her eyes were downcast, he knew them to be a lovely shade of ice blue. She fiddled with the cuff of her sleeve, her fingers hidden within the folds into which she'd tucked her hands. She looked the contradiction of strong and vulnerable— exactly as she had that first night he'd taken her home all those years back. The way that had clutched his heart and refused to leave his mind.

"Kate."

She stilled.

"You don't have to do this." Leaning elbows to knees, he cleared the rough emotion from his throat, still thinking about how she'd made him feel that first night. He'd wanted to protect her, to promise her that her life would work out, and she didn't need to be embarrassed about where she'd come from. And *he* wanted to be the one to make sure that happened.

In short, he'd wanted to rescue her.

How ironic was that? Now here they sat, both buried under the massive mess *he'd* created in his quest to be the hero in her life, and she offered to rescue him.

In a skoolie.

Could he live under that kind of humility? Not only living in a converted school bus—though that came with its own level of lower dignity—but could he handle living with her knowing not only had he failed on an epic scale at being her hero, but that she'd rescued him from being a homeless man on the streets?

Jacob had never been good at humility. All his life, he'd resented being overlooked—being cast into the shadows thrown by his brothers. He'd clawed through life trying to claim a place of his own, one of respect. Maybe even a position his brothers would envy.

"What else will you do?" Kate's quiet words seemed to speak straight into his internal battle.

He had no idea.

"This wasn't what I wanted for us. For you." Could she hear his sincerity in that? After last night's confrontation, it was clear that Kate thought him to be a selfish, arrogant man. Perhaps he was.

But at least part of his motivation had been for her, because contrary to what she believed, he loved her.

For better or for worse, he loved her. He just hadn't planned on worse.

ThisBoondockingLife entry #15

> *My husband needed some persuading before we stepped into this life. Actually, he was stunned into it, you could say. I announced to him this was what I wanted...and then told him I'd already made the purchase.*
>
> *Can you imagine his shock? I'll forever remember that expression—wide eyes, dropped jaw. Can't blame him—remember that I was quite the diva about Gertrude at first. It didn't take him long to come around though. Before long he was tying up loose ends for his business in Seattle, we were listing our luxury condo, emptying our closets of everything but what would be practical and would fit in 160 square feet of living space, and selling whatever we could that was left over.*
>
> *New life awaited us, and once he recovered from the whiplash change in our direction, we faced it together.*
>
> *Honestly, we had no idea what we were getting into. Ignorance is bliss?*

Chapter Nine

(in which a shaky new life begins)

Though life had felt cloudy for quite some time, this subdued climate between Kate and Jacob felt like sinking deeper into something that she was certain she'd never recover from. The feeling made her question nearly constantly her offer to him.

She'd had an easy out of this relationship. Easy, practically speaking anyway. But matters of the heart seemed to be ever muddied, ever complicated.

In the week since she'd discovered the truth about Jacob's business ventures and their collapsing lifestyle, Jacob had set himself to the messy business of bankruptcy. Kate didn't understand it all, other than to know that this would forever stain him, if even he could recover from the obvious humiliation he suffered from it all.

Within a matter of days, their high-priced vehicles were no longer theirs, their prime real estate condo was listed, and Jacob had arranged for a sale that would hopefully cover the debts owed on things like furniture and credit cards. Hopefully.

As far as the investment properties went, they were scheduled for auction, and arrangements were being made for Jacob's contractors to be paid...somehow. That seemed a mystery—Kate wasn't sure how that was going to happen. Not that she thought it didn't need to happen. It made her stomach twist to think that hardworking people wouldn't be paid what they were due because of her and Jacob.

It was startling to witness how quickly everything could go. It was heartbreaking to watch how this blow defeated Jacob. The man she had married had been determined and confident, maybe even to the point of arrogance. Her husband now walked with a shuffled gait, his shoulders curved inward, face cast downward.

All of it swirled a confusing mixed reaction in Kate. She resented that Jacob had done this, and worse, that he'd never told her anything about being in trouble. But also she knew a deep vault compassion, the kind that throbbed with ache for this man who had rescued her from a life she'd hated.

Exhaustion claimed Kate through the tug-of-war of emotions.

Jacob never told her anything at all about his business. She was to be the wife at home, looking lovely, conveying prosperity, and producing babies. At least, that was what it had seemed like. Jacob had never asked for her input, never involved her in his business affairs. He rarely involved himself in hers either. They'd basically lived separate lives under the same roof.

When she'd started writing, he merely shrugged at the idea. "If you'd like to try, Katie, go ahead." That was it, a passive, none-to-interested nod of permission. He had no idea how many novels she'd written (last count, 28). No idea how many she sold in a month. No clue what her royalties looked like. Up until the day after their world came crashing down, he hadn't cared.

Even now, he didn't ask much. But that was likely because he was too busy trying to contain the fires of disaster.

When irritation surged, threatening to overtake the tenderness she somehow still felt for him, Kate turned to her imaginary worlds. She heaped her emotions onto her characters, made them carry the burden. In that one week of chaotic changes, Kate wrote nearly a full novel, setting a new word-count record.

Jacob took notice.

"Do you make your heroes all the things you wish I was?"

Kate paused from a furious gust of words that blew from her mind through her fingers and onto her Word doc. Startled, she jerked her attention to the doorway of their bedroom. Jacob leaned against the frame, hands shoved into his sweatpants pockets, exhaustion etching every wrinkle of his furrowed brow.

Unintentionally, she met his despondent gaze. A sharp pinch radiated in her chest as she searched for an answer that wouldn't be a lie but wouldn't make things worse.

She couldn't find one.

One corner of his mouth twitched, like he was attempting to smile but just couldn't muster it. "You're doing pretty well, it looks like. I looked up your books. They sell."

She shrugged, swallowing against the tightness in her throat. "I do okay. Not as well as I wish."

"You write romance, right?"

"Yes."

He nodded, dropping his gaze to the shag rug on the floor. Then he rubbed the back of his head and rolled away from the doorframe until he stood. "Maybe I should read them sometime."

If he'd offered to read her work five years before, when she'd first started, Kate would have been ecstatic. Now...

Now she felt like he was hunting for faults. Shouldn't take him too long to find them. Not that she was ashamed of her work—she wrote sweet, clean romance. Stories in which, yes, she'd created heroes who, maybe, possibly were more like she wished her husband would be.

Attentive. Available. Completely captivated by the women they loved. And of course, successful.

Jacob would take all of that as a personal critique, especially now.

On a sigh, Kate closed her laptop, then let her head drop back against the headboard of their bed, a piece of furniture that would go to auction the following day, along with everything else. Things simply continued to spiral downward, and it seemed there was no way out of the ride.

She should have walked away, driven into some sunset alone. Just her and her laptop and that skoolie named Gert. It would have been easier.

***

Jacob rubbed his forehead just over his eyebrows. The headache was pounding its way through day number seven, with no end in sight.

He shouldn't have asked his wife that question. She'd looked so injured by it. Or maybe that was guilt? Either way, it hadn't made him feel better. It seemed to him, by the few Hallmark shows he'd watched, all romance stories were an exaggeration anyway, so it shouldn't have mattered. Shouldn't bother him.

Maybe if he thought his wife actually liked him, it wouldn't.

Once again, none of that mattered, because at this point her books were their salvation. *His* salvation—and he'd do well to remember that. Because of her, he would have a roof over his head, even if it was only the top of a school bus. Beggars couldn't be choosers, and he was an absolute beggar.

One who had approximately zero direction in his life at the moment. If not for Kate and this persistent, though irrational, pull she had on his heart, he'd simply wander off into the woods somewhere, hoping a bear or a cougar would have mercy on his wretched soul.

But Kate...

Though he'd failed her miserably, she owned his heart.

"Jacob?"

Hands still stuffed in his pockets, he turned from the window he'd been staring out and found her five feet behind him. She stood with her arms crossed, looking every bit as uncomfortable as he felt.

"I need to figure out how to get the skoolie. It's still in Oregon."

He nodded. Did she want his help with that? Or was she telling him that she was leaving again, this time no second thought? He cleared his throat. "Do you need me to do something?"

"I...I don't know how to get there now that we don't have vehicles. It's almost a five-hour drive."

Again, he nodded. "Past Eugene?"

"Yes."

"Do you mind if I call the guy you bought it from?"

Kate blinked, as if he'd surprised her. "Do you...I mean, with everything else you have going on, do you mind?"

"Not at all." The tension in his shoulders eased at the impression that she *wanted* his help with this. "If you'll show me his number, I can do it now."

She exhaled, the sound seeming one of relief. "I'll text it to you." Without waiting for his response, she scurried away.

Jacob watched her back until she disappeared into their room, suddenly wondering about this woman who'd been his wife for over seven years. She possessed this timidity that had called to him for rescue, and yet she owned a boldness he'd only seen glimpses of. Had that been because he hadn't been paying attention? Or was it a trait that only rose up in moments when she felt desperate? If that was so, then why? Why didn't Kate always move with boldness?

Who was this woman, and how on earth had he *not* come to know her in all the time they'd been together?

The phone in his pocket chimed. Filing his musing about Kate into a place he'd return to later, he lifted his cell and tapped the number Kate had sent him. After four rings, a man's voice came over the speaker.

"Bryce here."

"Hello, Bryce. My name is Jacob Murphy. I believe my wife purchased a bus from you."

A chuckle resonated from the phone. "Don't tell me you're calling to back out."

"No. Not at all."

"Awesome. You're gonna love it, man. It's a whole different kind of life. Just you, the woman you love, and anywhere you want to go."

Sounded like a romance story—entirely exaggerated. "Yeah. Well, we've already hit a snag with that. We're up in Seattle, and we're not sure how to get the bus here."

"Skoolie, man. If you're gonna live in one, you'd better call it by its preferred name. Which, come to think of it, is actually Gertrude. But she's a skoolie."

"Yeah, uh, where exactly did that name come from?"

"Which? Gertrude or skoolie?"

"Let's go with both."

Bryce chuckled. "School bus meets RV, man. Mash 'em up, you've got yourself a skoolie."

Of course. That made sense. Still, Jacob had a hard time picturing Kate and himself *living* in a skoolie. "Right. Got it."

"And Gertrude, just because. I painted her green, and Gertrude just went with green, I guess." Once again Bryce's voice wafted a carefree chuckle. "My wife says I'm especially unique."

Jacob could only imagine. "I'm guessing you're selling, uh, Gertrude, because you got married."

"Nope. Sally and I lived as man and wife in old Gert for two years. We had a blast. Dude, you're about to experience a whole different life. I'm gonna bet it'll be the best decision you've ever made."

"Yeah..." Wasn't really a decision. Carefree Mr. Bryce didn't need to know all of Jacob's woes though. "Look, I really just need help figuring out how to get Gert from there to here, because the thing is, we are currently without a vehicle. So do I Uber a trip that far? Catch a Greyhound? What do you suggest?"

"Oh man!" An image of a guy rubbing his hands together came along with Bryce's eager response. "Dude. Are you a big guy?"

"Uh, not especially." Jacob glanced at his reflection in the window. Most of his brothers were bigger-built men than he was.

"Perfect. I remember your wife is on the petite side."

"Does this have anything to do—"

"You need a Grom, bro."

"Come again?"

"A little Honda Grom. It's a bike. Sally and I had one. It fit perfect on the back of Gert. And here's the sweet part, buddy. I sold that little gem to a friend up there in Seattle. We chatted it up just last week, and he said he wasn't using it—thought he was gonna sell it. It'll be cheap, man. She's got a lot of miles on her, but I kept her *pristine*. She'll do the job."

This was starting to feel like a trip to a sketchy used-car lot. Who exactly had Kate dealt with here? "She will, huh?"

"Man, I totally read you loud and clear. This sounds like a setup. I promise you, it's not. I'm a God-fearing Christian brother, and I'd lose sleep thinking I swindled a man out of two bucks, let alone a grand."

Right. "Thing is, I don't have a grand to give anyone right now." If he had, he most likely wouldn't be dropping it on some used bike he didn't want in the first place.

"Listen, I'll work it out." For the first time in the conversation, Bryce sounded like a serious grown-up man. "You won't need to give Robbie anything. Just take the bike. You and your lady give it a ride down here to get old Gert, and then if you don't like the little rocket, you leave her with me. I'll square it with Robbie."

"You're..." Just take the bike, no money down. No collateral of any sort? Who did that? "You're not serious..."

"Totally, bro. I'll call Robbie."

Jacob's mind whirled. People didn't do things like that. Well, other than his parents, who could be generous to a fault. But they were the exception. In any case, this wasn't how business was done. This was how people got taken to the cleaners.

"You good with it, Jacob?" Bryce's grown-up serious tone remained.

"Uh, well, yeah. That'd be helpful. As long as I'm not gonna get pulled over somewhere between here and there and be accused of theft."

"Nope. Promise. I'll get some papers up there or something, if that'll make you feel better."

Papers? What kind of papers? That sounded either exceptionally ignorant or super fishy. Jacob didn't respond.

"I'll give Robbie a call right now and get back to you in a few. That'll give you and the missus a chance to jaw this out. Either way, I'm excited for the next phase of your life, buddy. It's gonna be an adventure you'll never forget—or regret."

Ha. Jacob was sure they wouldn't forget this *adventure*. Regret... He already had a thousand of those. What was one more to tack on?

The phone call ended, and Jacob looked for Kate. Not hard to find her—she'd propped up on the giant pillows on their bed, her laptop open again. She wasn't typing though, and by the despondent look on her face, she hadn't been writing at all for the past however long. Likely cause: himself. He'd discouraged her with his comment about her heroes.

"Hey," he muttered, trying to ignore the squeeze in his chest.

Kate didn't look at him. "Did you work something out?"

"Maybe." He hesitated, then dared to enter the room, lowering onto the end of the bed at her feet. "The guy, Bryce, that you bought the skoolie from? He's, uh, different."

"Yeah. He's pretty exuberant."

"Do you trust him?"

Those cool blue eyes met his, and something in them seemed to beg for his trust. "I think so. The people at the diner said he was a good person. And he's still holding my check, like he said he would."

Jacob nodded. "He suggested we buy an old bike of some kind

and use that to get down there. Said he had a buddy up here with one for sale. That seems...convenient."

"Is it expensive?"

"Relative to everything else we've ever bought? Not at all. But for us now?" He shook his head as a wave of defeat rushed over him yet again. "Might as well be that beach house we used to dream of."

"Then I guess it won't work."

"Bryce suggested we try it. Ride it down there and test it out. If nothing else, it'd be a means to get your skoolie. He said there'd be no commitment."

"That seems pretty generous, except didn't you say it was his friend's bike?"

"Yeah. Bryce said he'd square it. I don't know what that means."

Kate's lips seamed and her brow furrowed. After a long beat of silence, in which the sense of shared helplessness thickened, she looked back at her laptop. "Do you have another idea?" she whispered.

No. No, he did not. "I guess we pray for God's mercy."

She glanced up at him, as if his words startled her. Maybe they had. It'd been a long time since they'd prayed for anything, excepting the past couple of days.

Or perhaps that'd just been him.

ThisBoondockingLife entry #10

> *Our first night in Gert was a revelation. But it wasn't all glorious.*
>
> *My husband and I both grew up in neighboring small towns, so one would have thought that adjusting to the pulse and noise of the city when we'd moved to Seattle would have been the most challenging change of our lives. It wasn't.*
>
> *That first night was particularly dark—moonless as it was—and SILENT. I mean, ear-ringing silent. The kind that seems to come with a chill that has nothing to do with the temperature. I wondered, lying there in the smothering quiet of a night unlike any before known, if we'd made an epic mistake.*

Chapter Ten
(in which Jacob and Kate discover boondocking)

"We need to make a plan." Jacob lowered onto the wood-covered risers leading into the skoolie. By his slow movements and slight wince, he was every bit as sore as she was.

Turned out, riding a small sport motorbike for five hours could make one's body feel as if they'd been shoved into a tumble dryer and put on spin for a full day. Ouch. Every bone in Kate's body felt the vibration of that bike. Her legs ached. Back screamed. Arms trembled. And she'd just been the passenger on the back. Granted, she'd been the one to wear the hiking pack stuffed with things she and Jacob thought they might need for this trip, but still...

Jacob let out a low groan as he stretched backward. "Talking to Bryce... I don't know, Kate. We're not prepared for the life of a boondocker."

No, they certainly were not. How did one go from living in a luxury condo in the prime heartbeat of a hipster city to bus-dwelling vagrants? About as well as one shifted from a trailer queen to apparent wealth—that answer, in her case, had been not well at all.

Kate studied the length of Gertrude's green side. Twenty feet of metal and wheels. Eight feet of width. About 160 square feet of living and traveling space combined. Their condo had been well over 1,500 square feet, and often that amount of space had felt too small. How were they supposed to survive in 10 percent of the living area they were accustomed to, when it seemed they didn't even like each other?

Cautiously, she looked back at Jacob. "Do we have a choice?"

Jacob looked up at her with a studious expression, as if he was guessing her thoughts, and then let his discouraged gaze drift from her face to the scenery behind her. The acreage Bryce and Sally had inherited was rimmed with massive Douglas fir and ponderosa pines. Woven throughout the evergreens were many deciduous varieties—likely big-leaf maples and white oaks and ash—all on the brink of bursting forth with new spring life. The skoolie had been parked and leveled near the northern tree line, a hedge of something not yet leafed out obscuring the vision between where Jacob and Kate now deliberated and the old house Bryce and Sally were determined to restore. The distance and dormant vegetation offered a sense of privacy, allowing her and Jacob this moment of near panic in relative privacy.

"No, we don't have a choice—unless you want to kick me to the streets." He peeked at her again. "You could, you know."

He kept doing that. It unnerved her, because it was so unlike him. If they were going to do this, she needed him to pick up his head. Granted, he could definitely lose the all-business demeanor he'd held on to before, as it made him seem as if he thought himself superior to everyone, including her. But this defeated, useless attitude he'd replaced it with wasn't doing either of them any good. She needed him to participate, because heaven knew, she hadn't a clue what she was doing.

"You're right." Kate leaned a hip against Gertrude's cool frame. "We need a plan. A better one than what we've got. And I'm not a great planner, not a good detail girl. But details are your jam."

Staring at the trees, Jacob grunted.

Enough of this wallowing. "Jacob. We need a plan."

As he transferred his look to her, Kate thought she glimpsed a hint of determination flit through his eyes. She lifted a corner of her mouth, hoping it looked like encouragement.

"Bryce says he'd be glad to show us what they did." Jacob rubbed his palms against his jeans. "He suggested starting in the Coachella Valley in California—we'd be able to catch some of the early spring harvest, and the fact that it's warmer there would cut propane costs."

"Harvest?"

"I can work. Bryce even has a list of farmers and citrus grove owners who have offered seasonal employment in the past."

"Would you—" Kate caught her words before they tumbled out, biting her bottom lip. She tried picturing her husband, who preferred dress pants to those faded blue jeans, and button-downs to sweat-stained T-shirts, bent over in a field laboring for minimum wage. Honestly, she couldn't see it.

"Yes. I would. I need to work, Kate." His scowl folded deep on his forehead, and his blue eyes darkened. "Despite what you think of me, I'm not too proud to get my hands dirty. And it's not like I've never done manual labor before. I am a Murphy." The irritation on his face and insulted tone bit at her.

Yes, he was a Murphy. The one who hadn't liked chopping firewood and nailing in roof shingles. He'd wanted something else, and he hadn't been shy about letting everyone know it.

Into those thoughts, a sinking disappointment plunged through her—and it wasn't about Jacob. Not entirely, at least. Kate wondered when they'd become this. Rather than a couple determined to uphold one another, willing to believe the best of each other, they both felt the other saw the worst in themselves at all times. They hadn't always been like this, had they? Hard to say. With their relationship being so frowned upon once it had been made known, there had been an ever-present-but-never-discussed strain between them. She'd hoped they'd draw closer under the pressure. Clearly they had not.

What would happen to them in this tin can they were to call home? Talk about pressure—and nowhere to escape from it.

She didn't want to live that way.

Softening her gaze, Kate timidly reached toward Jacob until her fingertips brushed the thick waves of his sand-colored hair. "It sounds like a good plan."

His eyes pinched as he looked up at her, but then the hardness there softened. "The start of one. I hope, anyway. In the meantime, I talked with Connor. Our mail will be forwarded to him, and he said he'd ship the boxes I sent that way to us here. Bryce lent me their address." Hesitancy passed between them, and then he reached up to gently grasp her fingers. "I'll do what it takes, Katie."

She nodded, nose stinging at the soft use of her nickname. Maybe they wouldn't kill each other. Maybe...

Maybe they might even remember what it was like to like each other.

Or maybe that was simply the romance writer in her—always yearning for a happily ever after.

***

Jacob lay like a corpse. Cold and still.

It'd been a long time since he'd been this hyper-aware of his wife at his side. Sleeping in roughly half the bedspace they'd become accustomed to explained at least part of his rigid cognizance of her. Almost from the beginning of their rocky-start marriage, they'd had a king-sized bed. Moving down to barely a full-sized mattress, crammed into a cove-like area in the back of the skoolie, would take some getting used to, even if things had been well between him and Kate. Which they were not—and hadn't been in a long time.

And that was the other part of his tension, the bulkier part.

With every long inhale, Jacob breathed in the scent of the woman lying at his side. She was sweet and crisp in his breath, each draw touching on the still-living desire she'd awakened in him from their first kiss. Didn't help that as he shut his eyes, he remembered her every curve, the silk of her skin under his touch...

She'd been his Bathsheba, the beautiful woman he couldn't resist. The one he *should* have turned away and forgotten about.

At the thought, he muffled a groan and winced. Their story hadn't been *that* dark. He hadn't murdered anyone. It just felt like his relationship with Jackson was dead. That hadn't been healthy to begin with, so...

And he'd stopped short of *having* her before he and Kate were married. Barely. Even so, there was no adultery involved. Just the betrayal of his brother.

"Jacob?"

Jacob sucked in a sharp breath. Kate's sudden invasion into his tumultuous thoughts startled him. Pretending as if she'd woken him, Jacob sniffed. "Yeah."

"It's really quiet," she whispered.

Not in his head, it wasn't. But she didn't need to know that. "Yeah. Not like city streets, is it?"

"No swishing of cars. No sirens. It feels...empty."

Now he could relate. He felt empty, but that had nothing to do with the noise, or lack of it, surrounding them. "Sugar Pine is quiet."

"Yes, but not like this."

Jacob rolled his head on the pillow to face her. In the cloak of thick darkness, he could barely make out her profile as she stared up at the ceiling. "Are you scared?"

"Of the quiet?" Her voice wavered a touch.

"Of whatever is next?"

"Yes." The pillow beneath her head rustled, and then he felt her warm breath fan against his cheek. "Are you?"

All the years before, he would feign confidence. He never had wanted to show weakness, to appear timid. But all of that hadn't worked well for him, had it? Perhaps it was time for a new approach—a more honest one.

"Yeah. I'm scared."

The soft wisp of her inhale sounded. Then the warmth of her exhale brushed his face again. Jacob turned his face the opposite way. Beyond the large back windows of the skoolie, through which the brilliant pinpricks of white stars shone into a moonless black night, the *woot-woot-woot* of an owl shattered the overwhelming silence.

A touch, feather soft and wonderfully warm, grazed his forearm. Hers. A thrill of electricity ran up his arm where her fingers had just skimmed. Then her palm filled his. She twined their fingers together and simply held on.

Silence reigned again, this time even in his mind. Jacob closed his eyes and sighed. When sleep slipped him into gentle darkness, Kate's hand was still in his.

Chapter Eleven

(in which Jacob has an honest conversation)

"Señor Salazar owns this farm. His family also owns an orange grove, which, if you impress him, could help you in the late fall. He's no slacker, and if he thinks you are, you won't get a second chance." Pointing to an area on the map in Southern California, Bryce leaned over the rustic wooden table in the middle of the gutted front room of his home.

Jacob worked *not* to be distracted by all the undoneness of this house Bryce and Sally were living in while renovating. His need for tidiness nearly nullified his efforts at ignoring what felt like chaos. The man hovering over the table where he'd spread out several maps seemed entirely comfortable in the mess.

In personality, Bryce reminded Jacob of his older brother Matt. He possessed a unique combination of easygoing and determination. Obviously hardworking, but not over the top. Could balance work and play without much effort—and, in fact, mixed the two, as if that was the way life was supposed to be.

"But I think you won't need to worry about that, Jacob. Show up humble. Work hard. Don't complain. Those are the things that will impress him, and Salazar can be very generous when he's impressed." Bryce glanced up with an energized grin. "Man, I sort of wish I could go with you. The things you'll see and do!" With both hands, Bryce shook Jacob's shoulders. "You'll never be the same, bro. Seriously, this is going to change how you see life. You'll see creation like few ever get to. You'll experience the gift of work in a way that most men never fully grasp. Dude! You could spend your whole life never appreciating what work does for you here"—he tapped Jacob's chest—"but now? Now God's giving you this amazing chance to get a whole different perspective. Jacob! It's gonna be epic!"

Jacob struggled to paste on an expression that would pass for matched excitement. "Yeah. We're...stoked."

The brightness of Bryce's high-beam smile faded, and the man stepped back as he carefully studied Jacob. After an uncomfortable moment, Bryce shook his head.

"No, man. I don't think that's true." In place of shining exuberance, compassion passed over Bryce's expression. "You never dreamed of something like this, did you?"

Jacob looked away, pretending to study the open map on the table.

"How about Kate? This wasn't her idea, was it?"

"Well..." Jacob rubbed his neck. Going with that might salvage the thin bit of dignity he had left, and in a way, this *had* been Kate's idea. "She bought the bus."

"Skoolie." Bryce stepped closer again. "And the deal is, Kate didn't strike me as the skoolie kind of gal when I first met her. She still doesn't hit me that way. Jacob, I can handle the truth, man."

Likely that was so. Jacob was willing to bet there wasn't a whole lot life could throw at Bryce that Bryce couldn't handle. Man, to be wired that way. To be able to just go with whatever and be happy about it. As much as he could wish for that sort of personality advantage, Jacob simply wasn't built that way.

"The truth is"—Jacob stiffened his shoulders and forced himself to meet Bryce's watchful look—"we didn't plan this out." He motioned to the pile of maps strewn on the table. "Obviously. But it's what we're doing."

"Are you in trouble?"

Jacob held a stare on him that he'd practiced a million times with his brothers. Particularly with Jackson. It was his *back off and leave me alone* look.

"If we've got legal problems, man, then we have issues." Bryce frowned, and it looked both wrong and terrifyingly convincing on his usually upbeat face.

"Nothing illegal."

Bryce nodded, his expression immediately softening. "Then anything else is workable. Just tell me how I can help."

"This is helpful." Jacob motioned again to the maps.

"What about the Grom?"

"What about it?"

"If you're going to work while your boondocking, it'd be best if you had it. The places to camp aren't close to the farms. You could burn a whole lot of gas."

Pride bucked against admitting the truth, but there weren't a lot of other options. "I can't afford it, Bryce."

Not surprised at all, Bryce nodded. He readjusted his hat while looking up at the exposed rafters. "Here's the thing, buddy. I gotta get this roof dried in this week." With a smile back in place, Bryce looked at Jacob again. "I could use some help."

"Help?"

"I can even show you how to swing a hammer."

Clearly Bryce had no idea how Jacob had grown up. "I know how to swing a hammer."

"Excellent. Then you and Kate will stay."

"Stay?"

"Right where you are until the roof is done. After that, it's off on the best adventure you'll ever have. You, Kate, Gertrude, and the Grom."

"The—" Jacob swallowed. "You're giving me the Grom?"

"No. You're earning it. By roofing." Bryce stuck his hand out. "Deal?"

Staring at the offered handshake, Jacob froze. He knew what generosity was—his dad lived it pretty much every single day. But this...this was both humiliating and hopeful. Jacob had never wanted to be in this kind of position, one of need. But here he was, and Bryce's offer felt overwhelming.

Bryce closed the gap, reaching to pick up Jacob's right hand and shaking it. He waited for Jacob to meet his gaze. "There is dignity in this." A solemnness carried in his low tone. "I promise you, Jacob. There is always dignity in work."

***

Dirt caked Kate's fingers—wet, cold, and heavy. The softness of her hands would be but a memory after this day. Even with that, Kate wouldn't have done anything different.

Working beside Sally, Kate's knees sank into the damp black earth as she carefully crawled parallel the row Sally had lined out.

"My grandmother showed me how to garden in this very spot." Sally talked as she hoed another row, straight and long, to Kate's right. She'd been doing that all morning, chatting as she worked as if she and Kate were longtime friends. "Oh, what a glorious time we had! Nana loved the smell of the earth, and if she didn't get her hands dirty at least once a day, she thought she'd wasted her time. Goodness, she was quirky and fun."

Sally paused, leaning on her tool and lifting her face to the sky. Though clouds covered the blue, Sally grinned as if she felt the sunrays on her face anyway. Then she looked back at Kate. "Those Nantes are my favorite. In less than three months, we'll be picking carrots. Isn't that amazing? You put a seed in the ground, give it a dash of love and hope, and it gives you back something perfectly wonderful. I think everyone should try growing something at least once. Just to see the wonder of it all."

"It's like a prayer my nana taught me—she was Jewish. A messianic Jew." Sally's expression glowed. "But she held on to so many traditional Jewish practices, even after she believed that Jesus *is* the Messiah. Anyway, that prayer I was just talking about, it goes, *Blessed be Thou, Yahweh our God, king of the world who causes bread to come from the earth.* Isn't that just beautiful?"

Kate wondered if the young woman was out of breath. Wow, she was chatty. And super happy. About everything.

That struck Kate as so odd it was enviable. Maybe in a slightly annoying way, especially because Sally liberally salted her expressive conversations with Bible references and prayers and Jesus stuff. Not that Kate didn't believe in Jesus and God and all that. She did. From a dignified, let's not get carried away with religion sort of distance.

But this Sally woman talked about Jesus and God and the Bible like her whole life revolved around them. And she liked it that way.

Sally was, bar none, the happiest person Kate had ever spent any amount of time with. She also could produce the most words in a breath of anyone she'd ever met. And a startling percentage of those words were somehow related to God. Kate had no idea what to do with that. Be annoyed? Intrigued?

Jealous?

No. Certainly not jealous. Becoming quirky and over the top were not on Kate's list of personal ambitions.

Happy was, though.

"Kate?"

Suddenly Kate realized her hands were still, pressed into the chilled, damp earth and doing nothing. Worse, she'd stopped listening to Sally. "I'm sorry. My thoughts must have derailed me. What were you saying?"

Sally laughed. "Oh sweet sugar peas, if you only knew how often I get sidetracked! I can be talking about one thing, and two minutes later I'm off on something else and I have no idea how I got there."

Kate watched Sally as she shook her head and smiled. She had no idea what Sally had said before, and she ventured to believe that Sally didn't have a clue either.

Then the woman leaned the garden tool against her shoulder and clapped her hands. "I know," she said triumphantly. "I was asking you if you were ready for a break, that's what." She shivered, though it seemed forced. "It's chilly out here, don't you think? I've got cinnamon rolls and coffee in the house, and I'm dying to see what those boys have been up to all morning. How about that?"

Blinking, Kate couldn't help but feel like she'd just ridden a merry-go-round and couldn't quite right her footing. "Uh, sure? Should I finish getting the carrot seeds into this row?"

"Naw." Sally waved her off, lowered the handle to the hoe, and reached into her puffer vest pocket. "I've got this marker right here." She extracted a wooden popsicle stick. "We'll just jam it right into the spot you seeded last, and that way we'll know exactly where to begin again."

"Oh." Kate brushed her hands together. "Okay."

Sally did what she'd just described and then offered a hand to Kate. After brushing her knees to clear the black dirt, a mostly futile effort, Kate followed Sally to the house.

"I've almost perfected the art of baking using only the toaster oven. You'll get it too, I'll bet. That's the thing about living in such small spaces—you learn how to do with less. It's so amazing too, because living with less somehow makes you see how much you really have. It's like Paul telling the Philippians that he's learned how to live with plenty and with not much."

Walking next to Sally, Kate glanced at the woman.

"Know what I mean?" Sally said.

Kate had no idea.

Sally just smiled and continued on. "I'll write down that passage for you, and you could look it up, if you want. I turned to it so often when Bryce first took me out of my big-house, important-career life and made me a boondocker. Wow, that was some whiplash! I had no clue, and let me tell you, I was not entirely sure about the sanity of the man I'd married."

Wait, what?

"And I definitely had some questions about my own. Life's great like that, isn't it? You just don't know what you're missing."

Yeah, and Kate had definitely missed something. What had Sally's life been like before she'd met Bryce?

Chapter Twelve
(in which Jacob takes on a roof)

Jacob laid down his hammer on a secured shingle and ran his forearm over his brow, catching the sweat on his forehead just in time. Man, he hadn't missed this. The aching muscles in his back, shoulders, and arms. The filth that felt like tiny grains of sand covering his entire body. His brothers—Matt and Tyler especially—hadn't ever seemed to mind the construction life. Amend that: they'd loved it. Jacob had hoped he'd never have to go back to that sort of work.

Yet, up there on that roof, a warm spring sun spreading golden-white light over the treetops and the house he was currently on, Jacob focused on gratitude over his physical discomfort. Bryce and Sally had been exceptionally generous to Kate and Jacob over the past five days. So much that Jacob was certain this roofing job didn't even begin to cover it. They'd given them free parking—their boondocking life now underway in the Millers' backyard. They'd offered warm showers and hot meals.

And they'd welcomed Jacob and Kate as if they'd been lifelong friends, not complete strangers who had purchased their skoolie in a moment of pure desperation.

Who did that?

Well, his parents would have, Jacob felt sure. Dad and Mom were generous people, just like Bryce and Sally. Jacob was willing to bet that his married brothers and their wives probably were too. However, the reality on that was that Jacob didn't know his siblings well, so he couldn't say for certain. In general, they were better people than himself though, so it seemed like a reasonable assumption.

As a shrinking sense of less-than encroached on him, Jacob searched for a glimpse of his wife for distraction. A defense mechanism he'd perfected when he'd been young—ignore the hard feelings. Find something else to think about and hope the other things would go away. Things like feeling like the odd brother, the one who would rather solve puzzles and work Excel sheets than split firewood and play with power tools. Or worse, feeling like the easily overlooked one, or even the not-wanted one. The fun-hater. The too-serious-for-his-own-good party pooper.

The one always standing on the outside, never able to figure out how to fit in. And deeply resenting it.

He banished those inklings as he saw Kate emerge from the shelter of the tree line, a sapling of some variety in each hand. Tangled hairs of soil-darkened roots danced with the movement of their transport beneath Kate's dirt-speckled fists. Sally walked beside her, that ever-present joy lighting her face as she chatted every step of the way to a spot of turned soil that she and Kate had spent the morning working.

Watching Kate walk, listening with a hint of bewilderment in her expression, Jacob chuckled to himself.

"She's sure a talker," Kate had said about Sally three nights back, after they'd settled under the thick blanket on their tiny bed for the night.

"That would make two of them," Jacob had replied.

There had been a stretch of quiet then. Less tense than the normal silence that spanned what felt like a canyon between them lately. Then Kate said, "In a good way though. I like them."

"Me too." He thought on that—on why Bryce's exuberance didn't irritate him the way Jackson's usually had. There was a mystery there. One that cast a foreboding shadow in Jacob's already downcast heart. With it, there was a profound sense that Jacob would have to recon with it one of these days. Staring at the diamond sky that night, he pushed away that niggling warning and refocused on the conversation between him and Kate. After all, they didn't always share these kind of whisper-soft moments. Why ruin a rare gem with his inner turmoil? "They're both kind. Quirky, but kind."

"Yeah. Jacob?"

This talking thing that had germinated between them felt like a delicate new life. Jacob smiled into the night. "Yeah?"

"They're really happy, don't you think?"

"Seems so."

"Sally said she used to live in a big house. Had an 'important career.' Her words."

"Oh yeah?" He wouldn't have guessed that about their hostess. She appeared to be cut of the same cloth as Bryce—both hardworking, but neither the important-career type. Although, maybe that didn't mean what he had in his head, didn't mean completely absorbed and obsessive. Like himself. Ugh. He wasn't dealing with the turmoil right then...

"Yeah."

After Kate's simple, obscure response, a new quietness settled into the space again. Then, as had happened the first night they'd spent in the skoolie, Kate slipped her hand into his. He'd wanted to know what else she had been thinking, why she was pondering Sally's life. But her hand in his was...

Enough. It was like a silent wish shared between them. A fragile hope neither dared whisper for fear that it would shatter in the telling.

But it was there. He'd felt it and was convinced she had too.

On the roof, Jacob ran his fingers against the heel of his palm, remembering the simple, gentle warmth of Kate's hand in his as they'd drifted to sleep. Something was eroding in him, in a good way. For the first time in years, Jacob wondered what he would become if he submitted to whatever it was that was determined to reshape him.

"They're a pretty pair, aren't they, buddy?" Bryce's smiling voice startled Jacob from across the slanted roof. He didn't wait for Jacob's response before hollering to his wife. "Hey, good looking! How about you just find yourself a seat and watch me show off my skills?"

Shielding her eyes from the early afternoon sun, Sally looked up. "You're sure impressive."

Jacob looked back at Bryce to see how he'd respond. The man pushed up from his knees and struck a muscle-man pose.

"Woo, goodness. You'll make me swoon, sexy guy." Sally laughed and then waved her husband down. "Don't fall and break yourself."

Bryce continued to stand. "You're working too hard down there, pretty lady. Take a break."

"I've got trees to plant. Kate and I are putting in that orchard you and I planned."

"Kate, is my overly ambitious wife working you to death?"

At Kate's laugh, Jacob smiled full. Wow, it'd been a long time since he'd heard her laugh like that. All free and genuine and beautiful.

"No, sir. I'm having fun," Kate said.

Jacob didn't for one second think she was putting up a front. *This* was his wife—the true version of her. Where had she been the past seven years? How could he keep her?

"All right." Bryce removed his ball cap, ran his fingers through hair so sweaty that after it'd been tugged away from his scalp, it stood on end, and then he replaced the hat. "But listen, hot pants. Don't you get yourself worn out." He shook a finger toward Sally and then winked. "You and I have plans tonight..."

Oh good night. Heat flooded Jacob's whole self, and even from his spot way up on the roof, he could see Kate blush to the roots of her hair.

Sally simply rolled her eyes and walked toward the postage-stamp layout of her orchard. From the movement of Kate's shoulders, Jacob guessed his own wife was laughing.

He wished he was down there to hear it. And also, that maybe she and he had the kind of blushing romance and banter they'd just witnessed between Bryce and Sally.

At that thought, a sharp pain twisted in his chest. With their history and personalities, that seemed like too much to dream of. Especially now, when he'd lost everything, reducing their entire existence to life in a skoolie.

A life his wife would despise.

***

"You're going to do great!" A now-familiar mantra. Sally beamed at Kate from the opposite end of the narrow aisle in the skoolie. She'd been showing Kate a few tricks for making a simple hot meal on the single electric burner. "The dutch oven is a little piece of magic. Once you learn its secrets, you'll never go back."

"How did you learn?"

"Oh"—Sally waved the question off like it wasn't even a thing—"my grandmother, the one who lived here and taught me to garden."

"Oh."

Quick to spot discouragement, Sally crossed the minuscule space between them and gripped Kate's arm. "It's no big deal though. You'll figure it out."

"I'm not much of a cook in a real kitchen." Growing up on boxed dinners and frozen meals meant that she knew how to boil water and work a microwave. That was about it. After she and Jacob were married, takeout had been her jam. "I don't know how to live without a microwave." Or an actual shower that didn't require setting up at the back of this bus-skoolie thing. Or a toilet that didn't roll out from beneath their "sofa" near the front of the vehicle, and then incinerate whatever was deposited within. *Ew.*

She'd literally deceived her way out of trailer life because she'd hated it. How in all that was fair in life had she ended up here? *Maybe this is what's fair in life.*

"Aww, it's okay, honey." Sally tugged on Kate's arm to bring her into a hug. "You'll be okay. You and Jacob are gonna find your feet."

Kate hated that her eyes burned, and even more that she had somehow let down her armor in front of the exuberant, strangely likeable woman she'd only met a week before. Straightening her posture, she cleared her throat. "Well. I guess you figured it out." Stepping out of hugging range, Kate cast a puzzled look on Sally. "What was it you used to do? You know, that important career you had before Bryce made you a boondocker?"

Sally laughed. "I was a corporate accountant for a big pharma company."

"Truly?"

"Yeah. Hard to picture right? But I wore the pantsuits and heels, baby. Faithfully highlighted my hair so it'd look just so in my neat little work updos. Got a mani once a week. The full fast-track-successful-businesswoman deal."

"Were you successful?" Kate had learned that *looking* successful and actually being successful weren't the same thing at all. Thus this new life.

"Yep. I actually was. Made bank like a boss."

Kate's brows lifted.

"I hated it." Sally wore a serious expression for perhaps the first time all week. "Straight up hated my life. Can you imagine that? At twenty-seven years old, I was making six figures, ticked off all the boxes on my *dream big or go home* list, and was the envy of many of my friends. And I found out success could be empty."

"Why?"

"I'm still not too sure, but I think that there was always this idea of when I get this, then I'll be happy. You know, when I graduate, when I land the job, when I get the promotion, when I buy that big old bungalow... Like I thought happiness was a destination or something."

Wasn't it? Kate stood mute. Baffled.

"When I met Bryce, he was the happiest person I'd ever encountered. That's what grabbed me first about him. And it was so crazy to me, because at the time, he'd taken temporary work as a custodian at the corporate office, filling in for the man who held the job for twenty years, while he recovered from knee surgery. I literally met Bryce while he was mopping the hall outside the restrooms."

Mind blowing. What a story that must be.

"How did you go from corporate star to marrying a janitor?" Kate snapped her mouth shut as soon as the words were out, realizing what a snobbish thing that was to say.

Sally laughed. "A *homeless* janitor. Well, not homeless— *houseless*." She winked. "And long story short, he saw I was upset about something—honestly, I don't even remember what—and he bought me a cup of coffee. Next thing I knew, I'd agreed to a date. It was the most bizarre, wonderful date ever. He took me to his skoolie, parked near the beach, and fed me food he'd made in this very kitchen"—she motioned to the single electric burner on the counter—"and challenged me to count the stars. I'd never had such a relaxing, fun time in my life. Bryce was the kindest, most fun man I'd ever met. Three months of his energetic smiles, hopeful life outlook, and total faith in Jesus, and I was ready to leave life as I knew it behind."

"So Bryce is your happiness?"

"No." Sally's answer dropped hard and fast. She softened it with a tender smile. "No, Bryce is not my happiness. I mean, don't get me wrong. I'm ridiculously happy with him. But I think that I found out what he already knew: happiness isn't a destination. It's a choice. What will I do with my day? How will I spend my time? How will I treat other people? What will I do with the ups and downs that litter my path? Bryce, he chooses joy. It's a lifestyle. Happiness is what he brings along the journey, not a place he works to find."

That sounded like fairy dust. Maybe Bryce had never really hit the tougher parts of life? Maybe happiness was just easy for him. Which didn't help Kate a whole lot.

"Do you remember when I was talking about those verses in the Bible where it talks about being content in all things?"

Kate mentally scrambled to keep up with Sally's topic shift. Something she'd been doing all week. "Uh, sure."

"I wrote it down. Listen, in all seriousness, Kate, transitioning from my old life to Gertrude wasn't all smooth sailing. I cried sometimes. Missed daily, steaming-hot showers. Some days I even wondered if I was crazy for choosing that life. But there was such rich learning during that time. Truly, I discovered how much I'd attached my happiness to things, how heavily dependent I was on circumstances and others for my moods. Life outside of that was totally revolutionary." She withdrew a folded piece of paper from her back pocket and handed it across the space between them. "I guess what I'm trying to say is this: Bryce and I realize that you and Jacob didn't volunteer for this change in your life. For that, I wanna tell you that I'm really sorry. I'm so sorry that hard things have happened to you guys. But, well, maybe this sounds completely trite to you, but I really believe it: what maybe seems like the worst thing ever can turn into the biggest blessing of your life."

"How?"

"Because you decide to make the best of it. No matter what."

Sally was right—that sounded thoroughly trite. The thing was though, the woman was completely sincere. And happy.

The other thing was, Kate was sick of being miserable. Perhaps trite was worth a try.

***

The chilled fog held the house in a thin veil. As Jacob neared the skeleton of the back porch, he could make out Bryce's figure, reclined in an Adirondack chair. It was the first time Jacob had really observed Bryce truly being still for more than eight seconds at once, but even so, an energy pulsed from the man.

What was it about him that fueled this...this whatever it was? Hyperactive? Perhaps. Bryce could fall under that category. But the substance of the man wasn't simply that. There was depth and purpose to Bryce's energy, a quality that made him inspiring rather than exhausting.

The thick white mist dissipated as Jacob quietly stepped on the first of two risers to the porch, clearing the view. Bryce looked up from the thick book lying open on his lap.

"Morning, neighbor." He lifted the mug in his right fist, the steam of whatever was contained therein leaving a wispy trail in the air.

"Morning." Jacob crossed the unstained decking. He motioned

to the book. "Am I interrupting?"

Bryce grinned in his easy, welcome way. "I'll finish in a few minutes, but you're welcome to sit, if you can handle a shared silence."

Silence with Bryce? That seemed nearly a contradiction—one that piqued Jacob's interest in a way that almost made him want to make a bet against Bryce's ability to do it.

"Fresh coffee in the kitchen, if you'd like." Bryce motioned toward the front door. "Help yourself."

Huh. Maybe Bryce would bet against himself too. Suppressing a chuckle, Jacob nodded and redirected his path to the door. "I'll take you up on that."

Warmth wrapped around Jacob's chilled body as he passed into the Millers' home. At the hint of a fresh brew, Jacob inhaled. Warmth and coffee, such small luxuries he'd never appreciated quite like this. A stab of conviction nicked deep within, but rather than fighting it or denying it, Jacob surrendered to the knife. If he needed heart surgery—and all indicators pointed to a *yes* on that—then let the surgery begin.

Pressing into that pain, Jacob walked through the house to the kitchen. Even into the dull, aching throb that the cut of conviction had brought, an underlying sense of peace held him. He thought of Kate, wrapped up in the bundle of blankets and quilts in the skoolie. *Katie...* Her name was a cry and a hope. He'd promised her a much better life than this, but at his worst failing, she'd not abandoned him. That still didn't make sense, especially since she clearly had thought to. Why had she changed her mind in the moment of finality?

Jacob knew he hadn't deserved it. Could it mean that he was more to her than a ticket out of the trailer park?

Katie... He'd hoped to truly win her heart with his success. It seemed all hope for that was gone—but she was not.

Katie... Standing at the counter, Jacob spread his palms flat against the cold stone and leaned against them. She filled his mind, her dark lashes spread against creamy skin, soft mouth slightly parted. What did she dream of now that their plans had come crashing down around them? Jacob shut his eyes and sighed. He hoped she was warm and her sleep was sweet. Maybe he'd take her a mug of piping-hot coffee. Would she smile at him if he did? A lightness filled his chest at the thought.

For now, he poured himself a mug and wandered back to the front porch. Bryce was just closing his book—a Bible, Jacob was fairly certain. A memory long pressed into his mind surfaced, and Jacob easily pictured his dad sitting there on that chair, head slightly bowed, eyes closed. Praying over the day and the people God had placed on his heart.

As the image in his mind morphed into focus on the truth of who was there—that it was Bryce, not Dad—a dart of homesickness pinged Jacob's heart. It'd been years since he had felt free enough to sit and have an honest conversation with his dad. Too many years, and suddenly the longing for Dad's calm wisdom and fatherly input made Jacob wince.

"Is it too bitter?"

Jacob's attention snapped to Bryce. "What's that?"

"The coffee. Did I brew it too strong?"

"Oh." Jacob chuckled and lowered onto the chair next to Bryce. "No, not at all."

"You made a face."

The need to open the vault of his heart pressed hard. "Can I ask you something?"

"Yep." Bryce crossed an ankle over his knee and sat back.

"All this..." Jacob waved a hand over the porch, the house, and the acreage they faced. "Was this the goal eventually?"

"For me? No."

"Sally?"

"Actually, no, not for her either. She was on a fast-track course for corporate success. And I liked life on the road."

"But you're not mad about it? I mean about being here, about losing your dream?"

Bryce sat forward, his well-used laugh soft. "I *lived* a dream, buddy. I didn't lose it. Now, I'm living a new one—one I didn't plan on or think up. Life's full of twists and turns, you know. You either ride it with a smile or you resent it. I'd rather ride, myself."

Staring into the thinning fog, Jacob nodded, though he wasn't sure he really could relate. The orange strength of the sun seeped over the tips of the trees hemming in the acreage, the color itself warm. Light caught the mist and dew, scattering the panorama with a thousand diamonds.

"Did you lose a dream, Jacob?"

He couldn't turn to look at the man asking. Jacob nodded. "All of them, it seems. It's like I keep grasping, and..." He didn't finish.

"A man aptly named..."

Jacob didn't know what that meant exactly.

"God sometimes pries our fingers from the things we clutch the hardest so that we have open hands to receive what He longs to give us."

A flash of resentment rose up, and Jacob glanced toward the Bible Bryce had laid on the railing in front of them. "I don't remember reading that in the Good Book."

"Probably because it's not there. Sally told me that once. I think she could relate to your struggle right now. She had some big dreams that she ended up letting go."

"For you?"

Bryce shrugged. "Yes and no. I think more for herself, because she needed to. I was just the nudge."

"What do you mean, she needed to?"

"The pursuit of success consumed her. All her waking thoughts, even some of her dreams, she couldn't escape it, and it made her exhausted. After a while, she resented what she'd once thought would make her happy. Bottom line? She was miserable."

Sally wasn't miserable now—there simply wasn't a question about it. She shared her husband's zeal for life, even if she wasn't as high energy as Bryce. She was happy. They were happy.

Once again Jacob moved his stare from the now sun-soaked field that extended toward the tree line to the Bible resting on the railing. "Do you read every morning?"

"I do."

"Does it help?"

"Not sure how to answer that. Help me succeed? I don't know. I'm not sure our definitions of success are the same, Jacob. But listening to God's letter to man every day, it reminds me of what this life really is, who I really am, and ultimately what my goal is."

The statement begged for clarification, but Jacob didn't feel ready to ask. "My dad reads every morning too. Always has, for as long as I can remember."

"Are you close?"

"To my dad? Not really."

Bryce held a long look on him, and Jacob felt both his compassion and a penetrating understanding that made him uneasy.

"Why not?"

With both hands, Jacob gripped his half-empty mug, the warmth seeping into his hands losing strength. "It's complicated."

Smoke and mirrors. That was all that was. Jacob knew the truth. Yeah, life as a misfit Murphy could be complicated. That was the reason he wasn't close to most of his brothers. He didn't understand them, and he felt misunderstood by them. But that wasn't why he was estranged from his dad.

Jacob was ashamed. That was the real reason—it was that simple. And that hard.

ThisBoondockingLife entry #1

> *The road winds forward like a scrolling invitation. "There is adventure ahead," it whispers. "I dare you to try something new."*
>
> *We are answering that invitation.*
>
> *My name is Kate, and I'm married to Jake. Together we are starting a new chapter of life—a boondocking life. Over the past month, we moved out of our luxury condo, sold nearly everything we own, bought an adorable skoolie (that's a school bus converted to an RV, for those who don't speak the language yet), and have charted a new, hopeful life plan.*
>
> *We didn't expect this, but now that we're driving that green bus, lovingly tagged "Gertrude" by her previous adventurers, the anticipation is building.*
>
> *What will this boondocking life look like?*
>
> *I'm glad you've asked, because Jake and I are about to find out. Consider this your open invitation to our adventure. I'd love to take you along.*

Chapter Thirteen

(in which the road trip begins)

They had a plan.

Kate reminded herself of that fact as Jacob guided Gertrude down the highway. Eventually, they'd have to find their way over to the interstate and brave that new and terrifying world, but right then, all Kate would allow herself to think about was the fact that they had a plan. That way all her fears wouldn't send her into a hyperventilating panic.

At the threat of such, Kate opened the Excel tab on her laptop and looked over the spreadsheet Jacob had created during the evenings while they were camping in the Millers' backyard. She examined yet again the columns and rows of expenses and hoped-for income.

He'd asked—with more humility that she'd seen from him in ages (excepting the past few weeks), if she thought they could live off her royalties. As a sensation of truly being needed, new for her in this marriage, lifted her heart, Kate had gone over the numbers for her books. She wasn't the spreadsheet guru Jacob was and hadn't tracked her expenses versus true net gain very well, but over the course of a few hours, Jacob had what seemed to be a decent handle on what she predicted. All of that he'd plugged into a tab labeled *Kate's Earnings* on the spreadsheet he'd created.

And he'd been impressed. "Wow, Katie," he'd whispered. "I had no idea you were doing this well."

Well was relative. If she'd been doing that well, they wouldn't be resigned to a life in a converted school bus, would they? Even still, by Jacob's figures and hopes, if they were super careful and really stingy, they could make ends meet on her net royalties.

Stinginess aside, there was a tremendous sense of grateful accomplishment in that. She was *needed* and she was able to make meaningful contributions to their life.

From there, Jacob had conjectured what he could earn during the next month or so as a seasonal picker in the Coachella Valley—all based on what Bryce had shared and advised. Those figures had been plugged into a separate tag labeled *Jacob's Earnings*, and what he cautiously hoped for would double what Kate could contribute.

"Do you really think that'll happen?" Kate had asked, frightened to hope for it.

"Bryce says if I work hard, stay humble, and treat everyone like friends and family, I'll find a place that will be good to me. He says if I work like I did with him, we'll be fine." Jacob had paused there, looking at his work-roughened hands. After six days of laying felt, hammering down shingles, and working at it for as long as daylight would allow, his knuckles had cracked and bled. Even so, his expression whispered *unworthy*, and Kate had known he was really struggling with the issue of the small motorcycle—the Grom—that they were taking with them.

Bryce had said Jacob earned it, and he'd already squared it with his friend in Seattle. Jacob clearly didn't agree, and Kate knew why. The Millers had been unbelievably generous to them—free parking, food, hot showers, and buckets of advice. Kate and Jacob both knew that little Grom was basically a gift. An undeserved token of grace from people who had no real reason to give it all.

That had affected her husband. Deeply.

Jacob had blinked and cleared his throat, glancing at her with apprehension. "Kate, if we can really make it off your book earnings, I'd like to send whatever I make to my contractors. They really got shafted because of my failure."

He knew down to the penny how much the people he'd hired to work for him *hadn't* gotten paid, even with the settlement. People with families and bills of their own. In that quiet, strained moment sitting across from him at their pull-out table in Gertrude the night before, Kate had felt a tender emerging of the respect for her husband that had severely atrophied over the years. With a burn in her eyes, she'd looked to her hands and nodded.

"Please don't be angry..." he'd whispered.

He'd misread her emotions. Seemed he'd done that often over the years. It pained her to realize how much they'd both misunderstood each other throughout their marriage. Kate looked up, catching his eyes. "I'm not."

She couldn't say more, and after a long-held look, Jacob nodded and went back to the numbers.

As ever, her husband had been meticulous with his figures, a fact that made Kate wonder for the hundredth time what on earth had happened with his business that brought them to total ruin. Jacob wasn't a careless man. Driven—absurdly so—yes. But not reckless, especially with data. She'd witnessed this truth about her husband even during the foreclosures and the process of filing for bankruptcy. Jacob had tracked everything down to the last penny, knew exactly how much he still owed—and would likely never be able to repay. How did a man with that much awareness get himself into this big of a disaster?

Kate had a quiet, sickening suspicion that the driving force behind Jacob's failure had something to do with her. That very much made his shame her own.

"Second thoughts?" Jacob's quiet voice drew Kate's attention into the present and away from her laptop to where he sat at the giant steering wheel guiding Gertrude into their new life. His gaze was fixed forward on the quiet highway, but for a flicker of a moment, he glanced up at the long mirror above the windshield and met her eyes.

Kate winced but pushed into honesty, which was not a habit she'd practiced over the years when it came to how she felt. "A million of them. Still."

"Me too."

"But as you said, what other choice do we have?"

Again, his glance met hers in the mirror, his thoughts bleeding through his folded brows. *She* had choices. She had an income, slight though it might be. *He* was the dead weight here.

She knew intimately how such impressions of oneself sliced deep, and despite their many struggles, Kate didn't want Jacob to suffer under it. "You'll find work. Whatever happens next, we're in it together."

The strain above his eyebrows eased, allowing a touch of gratitude to filter into his expression. "I was thinking last night about your writing. Have you thought about a blog?"

She shrugged. She'd tried and failed at least a half dozen times. When it came to blogging, she simply felt she had nothing worthwhile to say. The only interesting thing about her was that she had imaginary friends. That worked for books, but not necessarily for blogging. "A few times. They're not as popular as they used to be, so you have to be really good at it to succeed. I don't have anything to write about that would cut through the noise."

"What about this?" Jacob patted the dashboard.

"Gertrude?"

"Well, yes, that. But boondocking. Not everyone is doing it, right?"

Hmm...

"What would I say?"

"Whatever you want. You're the writer. From all appearances, a pretty good one."

Kate molded a small smile at his compliment. Inside, she cringed at the stab of disappointment about the fact that Jacob had never once read any of her work. Granted, she wrote romances, not really Jacob's genre of choice. Still, she was his wife. It would be nice if he'd shown some interest in what she did.

"I think you could make something out of this weird new life we've fallen into."

He was showing interest now, right? Yeah, because their livelihood depended on it. *Decide to make the best of it.* Sally's smiling voice invaded Kate's bitter thoughts. *No matter what.*

Easier said than done. Kate drew a quick breath. "I'm not good with SEO and design."

"What's SEO?"

"Search engine optimization."

Jacob nodded, thought lines creasing his foreheads. "I'm not sure what that means, but it sounds like it's not really writing related."

"Yeah. It's more about metadata and ranking with search engines. Stuff I'm not good at."

"Would I be good at it?"

"Likely."

"If I did some research, could I help you?"

Kate shifted her gaze from Jacob's face in the mirror to the road ahead of them. They'd merged onto a southbound highway a while back, traveled through intermittent sections of heavy pine and wide-open brushy plains. The Fremont-Winema National Forest was a kaleidoscope of sharply carved mountain peaks, stretches of ancient, time-eroded volcanoes, blue-green lakes, and rich green forests—some sadly damaged by unmitigated beetle infestation. Ahead, nearly covering the expanse of the valley they approached, held the width of a smooth cerulean body of water. The Upper Klamath Lake, whose size alone was breathtaking, but on this clear day, under an unblemished cobalt sky and with glass water that perfectly mirrored the tree-covered hills that created its boundary, the sight became one that Kate would not soon forget.

The contrast of expansive water and the triumphant hills that surrounded it seemed something like Jacob and herself. Opposites, bound together.

Kate considered Jacob's offer to help, and the thought made her gut quiver. Would that even work? They were barely making it as a married couple. Was it relationship suicide to try to work together?

But Jacob was good with numbers. Loved data. Loved tracking things and figuring out systems. Kate was terrible at those things, and she hated them, which made it unlikely that she'd ever get good at them. Honestly, spreadsheets were more likely to give her a case of heartburn than to make her smile.

"You won't dictate what I write?" she asked in return to his question.

"I'm hardly in a position to dictate anything to you, Kate. Don't think for a moment that I'm likely to forget why we live in a skoolie now."

At his low, contrite voice, Kate immediately wished her words, and her attitude, back. This was not exactly deciding to make the most of anything, was it? She looked back at the mirror, finding that her frowning husband was focused on the pavement on which they traveled.

Once again, her attention traveled back to the oncoming mass of beauty. Those mountains, that lake, both held the potential within themselves to destroy the other. But together...

Wow. Together, they were stunning. Complementary in their strengths and complete in their beauty.

"We'll try it then," she said, forcing cheer into her voice. "I'll work on some entries while you drive. Maybe we can make something out of it. Together."

Kate breathed deep, willing encouragement into the place that felt disquiet. Perhaps this project would be the key to making the best of this new life.

***

Nine hundred and thirty-ish miles.

Jacob secured the gas pump back into place, feeling the hard *cha-ching* of the total amount charged for filling up old Gert all the way down to his shoes. That was it for them for the month—they'd spent almost $300 in gas getting from Oregon to the Coachella Valley. It was actually over the regular monthly allowance he'd figured for this "adventure," but Bryce had assured him that it was both necessary and worth it.

Stay at least six weeks, and you'll be shocked at how much milage you can get out of the Grom. Once you park, stay there for as long as you can. Most boondocking locations will allow for fourteen days. A couple down there go up to thirty, as long as that's it for the calendar year. Don't fudge those rules. Seriously, bro. Just don't. You'll ruin it for everyone. Not cool.

Jacob had felt uneasy about going that far on their first stretch, but he needed the steady work. His next opportunity for steady work wouldn't open up until early June—if he landed the seasonal position at either Yellowstone or the Grand Canyon. That was a wide-open if. Either way, that left nearly half of May as a gap in his income, which wasn't comforting. Since Bryce had lived this way before, Jacob felt he had little choice but to trust the man. Still, going over budget their first month out...

This is how I lost everything. Exactly what got us into this position in the first place.

"Fill up?" Kate hopped from the street she'd crossed onto the sidewalk near the filling station, a loaded canvas shopping bag weighing one shoulder and another dangling from her hand. A gust of wind coming off the cloud-covered mountain range tossed her blond hair across her face, but she shook the tresses away, unbothered.

"Filled up," he said. "We're stuck here now. That was pretty much all our fuel money for the next few weeks."

She nodded. "That was expected, right?"

Pressing his lips together, he jammed his hands into his pockets. "Yeah." He nodded toward the bags. "How'd grocery shopping go?"

Kate grinned. "I followed Sally's list to a *T*. Even found some things on sale and came in under budget."

Her blue eyes sparkled, as if she'd just won a game or something. Seeing her handle this so well was both massively unexpected and encouraging. One corner of Jacob's mouth poked up. "So you win this round, I guess."

She laughed. Like she had with Sally, Kate laughed. At him. Suddenly he didn't loathe this whole situation quite so thoroughly. Meeting her before she reached Gert's door, he reached for the bag gripped in her hand. After she surrendered it, he slid the other from her shoulder. "Will this food stretch, do you think?"

"Sally helped me with a menu. We won't be eating lobster and steak anytime soon, but we won't get scurvy either. Especially if we can find some seconds to purchase later on." Kate tipped her chin, flashing him a sassy look. "That one's on you though, since you're going to work the farms."

"Got it." As Jacob followed her up the steps into their skoolie, he wondered at her bright attitude. This had become a challenge to Kate at some point along the way. And now she was challenging him. Her grin said *Play the game, Murphy. Let's just play this game.*

He kind of liked that, even if his gut knotted with the unknown. He liked seeing a sprout of optimism and life take root in his wife. It'd be helpful to have it nestle in his own heart as well.

God, if you're not done with me, I sure could use some help here...

Lowering the canvas bags onto the seat that had been anchored against the side wall of the bus, Jacob unloaded the dry staples. He handed Kate a huge bag of rice, two good-sized bags of dried black beans, a canister of bulk oatmeal, a ten-pound bag of flour, and a five-pound bag of sugar. From the other bag, he caught sight of dried fruit, several spice jars, a large jar of peanut butter and another of jam, two cartons of eggs, a small jug of milk, and a bag of bread.

That was it.

"This will get us through the month?"

"Some will last the month. I still have a weekly allowance set aside for things that won't keep. And you're going to get us cheap produce, remember?"

"Right."

The pressure clamped harder. *Lord, I really need to find a job. Please let that Salazar man take pity on me...*

Kate finished putting staples in the long cabinet above their tiny air-fry oven, and the cold stuff into the dorm-sized refrigerator. She worked like she had a plan, which made him proud of her. Generally, she didn't create a strategy, so he knew this took effort on her part.

Truth was, Kate had been really working at this whole thing. He really couldn't stand the thought of letting her down again.

More pressure.

Lord, please...

"Done. How about that—it took less than three minutes to put groceries away." Kate turned around, still wearing her grin. It faded, however, when she took him in. "You okay?"

No. No he wasn't. This wasn't okay. He'd promised to get her out of the trailer park, to give her the life she'd been desperate enough to deceive for. Now...

Now she was standing in front of him desperately trying to make the best out of living in a converted school bus. Because of *him.*

Defeat threatened to flatten him. Where was that seed of optimism Kate had found?

"Jacob?"

He looked away, rubbing his heated neck. "Yeah. I was just

thinking that I'd like to check in with Salazar Farms before we go find the park Bryce recommended. It's away from the valley, and I'd like to secure some work before we go."

Hesitation made her brow furrow, and she leaned to look out the windshield. "The clouds are pretty heavy out there. Do you think we should try to find a place to park this beast before it rains?"

He'd thought the same thing when they'd first rolled into the valley. But he wouldn't sleep tonight without knowing he'd have at least a start on a small way of righting their lives. "I looked up the climate around here. This time of year it only rains like once a month at most."

Jacob bent to look out the window as well. The view he took in was an odd contrast of things that didn't fit together in his mind. Tall palm trees lined the streets, but yards were mostly xeriscape with rocks and what he thought of as desert plants—shrubby sage, spikey yucca. From that there were bright spots of rich green—lawns that were certainly watered routinely—and in the distance a large expanse of a pristine, manicured golf course. The backdrop to it all: the imposing upsurge mountain ranges that engulfed the valley. The San Bernardino Mountains to the north and east, and to the north and west, extending south, were the San Jacinto and Santa Rosa Mountains. What was mostly desert in this wide basin held a vital secret of fertile, well-drained soil that was unlocked by the life-giving waters of the Colorado River by way of irrigation. The result was a collision of vastly different landforms and climates all surrounding the bed of an ancient lake.

The summits of the mountain ranges were now blocked from view as the thick gray cloud cover had crawled over the heights, then sagged heavy overhead. Everything about it warned of rain—the weighted feel of the air, the cool stirring of wind that rocked the fanned tops of the palms, even the smell in the air. But once set, Jacob didn't often change his mind.

"I think the odds are in our favor," he said, moving toward the driver's seat. "I mean, what are the chances that we've arrived on the one day it rains?" He flashed a grin he knew was not at all confident.

Kate pursed her lips, lifted a brow, and then sat on the bench near the exit. Her silence pulsed with disapproval.

***

The odds may have seemed in their favor, but reality certainly had not been.

Kate leaned back against the cream-colored softness that covered what had surely been an olive-green pleather bus seat, tipping her head against the closed window so that she could watch the laden sky weep.

Jacob had been wrong. Again.

Somehow she'd gone past angry. A month ago, she'd have been livid, and they would have had a strapping argument about it. But after years of high-energy conflicts, all Kate found left in her tank was a sinking resignation. Perhaps that was for the best.

The downpour clattered against the metal roof of the bus with relentless consistency, just as it had for the past hour. So loud and steady was the sound, Kate didn't hear the whoosh-squeak of the door opening, and she jolted nearly off her seat when her soaked husband popped into her view.

"Hey." Water matted his sandy-blond hair to his head and ran tiny rivers down the sides of his face and his nose.

Inhaling deeply, Kate recovered herself, found a towel in a side cabinet beside their closet—a small box of a thing that didn't actually deserve the title—and handed it to Jacob. "Well?"

"Took Salazar a while to see me. He'd been out in the fields to help his hands hurry up with what had been harvested."

"And?"

Jacob looked away, his expression not too promising. "They start at five. He said to show up, and we'll see."

"Five in the morning?"

"Yes. First shift gets done before the heat of the day. Says the produce is better that way."

"But he didn't say yes for sure?"

He looked to the puddle at his feet. "No. Said first thing was to see if I'd show up. He...he didn't seem too impressed with me."

"Why?"

"I think he assumes I'm a lazy man who thought picking vegetables would be an easy, mindless task." Finally, Jacob looked back and met her eyes. He watched her, searching for something she wasn't quite sure she could give him.

Reassurance. That he wasn't that man.

Jacob wasn't lazy. He was an excessively driven man. But this kind of physical labor wasn't his thing.

"Why do you think he thought that?" Kate evaded the pleading of his look.

With a shrug, Jacob finished drying himself off. "He asked if I knew what it was like to bend over plants for six to eight hours straight. If I thought my *blanco* back could take that kind of strain. He also made a point to tell me they didn't take water-cooler breaks."

"Oh." Kate stared at the shoes he kicked off and put under the dashboard.

"I won't quit, Kate."

She glanced up to find him scowling. "I didn't say anything."

"I *can* work. I grew up working—doing physical labor."

"I know that, Jacob." Why did he suddenly turn so fiercely defensive?

The quiet between them took on a hard edge, and Jacob whipped the towel over the driver's seat and then dropped onto it. After another razor-edge beat, he sighed. "He also advised me not to drive toward the national forest, where we planned on staying tonight. Said it was likely under flashflood warnings, and the roads would be six inches of mud."

"Oh no. Then what?"

"There's a spot closer. We'd still park on dirt pack—which is likely now mud, and there's no facilities at all. But it'd just be for the night. Salazar seemed to think the roads would dry up by midday tomorrow."

"Okay."

"I didn't know it was going to dump like this, Kate." Defense still rang hard in his voice.

How could he have thought otherwise? The storm had come off the mountains like a thick wave, clouds full of moisture and air a ready warning of the storm.

But Kate still wasn't up for a fight. Not when the only option either of them had at the moment was to remain in this tiny living space together.

"I guess we're especially lucky." She tried on a wry grin.

Jacob shook his head and gripped the steering wheel. He muttered something under his breath. Kate thought she heard the word *dumb* in there. But he reached for the keys in the ignition, started the rumbling engine of the bus, and carefully wove his way back to the highway that had brought them to the Coachella Valley.

So far, this boondocking life was going swimmingly.

Thisboondockinglife entry #2

> *With every new adventure, there will be a
> steep learning curve. The key is to refuse the
> impulse to surrender. A very close second key
> is to learn from mistakes. Ideally, you could
> learn from others' mishaps (thus this entry—
> and you're welcome). Or you can go out and
> find your own messes. (That's bound to
> happen, so reread the first key. Memorize it.
> Embroider the words* No Surrender *on a
> throw cushion and add that little piece of
> luxury to your tiny living space.)*
>
> *With that, I deliver to you that which we
> have learned: under wet conditions, in
> unexplored terrain, stick to the pavement. Do
> this, and it will go well with you.*
>
> *Ask me how I know.*

Chapter Fourteen
(in which Gertrude gets stuck)

It'd gone from bad to worse, which was super frustrating since the day—this trip, actually—had started off with the first glimmer of promise Jacob had felt in weeks. Years, even. Was it too much to hope that life would stop spiraling out of control at some point in the near future?

At the moment, with one side of Gertrude's back end sunk in a murky hole of slick mud, leaving her top side slanted at a telling angle as the darkness of night swiftly closed in, it seemed that yes, it was too much to ask for things to go steadily toward the better end of life's experiences.

Jacob smashed his palm against the metal side of Gert's

exterior.

"We can just stay like this," Kate said as she hung halfway out the open bus door.

"That should make for a good night's rest."

"What else are we going to do?"

He could have listened to her in the first place. Actually, Jacob could have listened to Kate several times during the past few hours, and this whole mud fiasco could have been avoided. She'd wanted to go find a decent place to set up camp before it'd rained. He'd decided to get ahead of the morning and secure a job. *Lotta good that did.* She'd not wanted to back into this parking spot where they'd spend their first night in the valley, suggesting that they just park parallel since clearly no one else was sharing the space that evening. He'd wanted to back it in and make it look like they knew what they were doing. So he backed Gert up...right into a sink hole. *Nice going, smart guy.*

There's an art to doing life together. His father's voice intruded into his memory. *There's a delicate line between being determined and stupidly stubborn. Usually arrogance is the boundary, son.*

Nearly twenty-eight years old, and clearly Jacob hadn't learned that yet.

Tipping his head back, the weak end of what had been a gusher of a storm softly splattered against Jacob's face. To the west was a narrow slit of lighter gray between the velvet blackness of the mountain range and the heavy darkness of the cloud-covered night. Within an hour, Jacob guessed, the sky would clear and they'd glimpse a star-studded valley dome.

"We'll wait a bit. The rain's letting up, and it'll clear."

"And?"

"Hopefully, the ground will firm up."

"In an hour?"

Man he sure hoped so. Jacob shrugged. "Maybe."

"Okay. Supper?"

"Can we make anything with the bus all catawampus like this?" Kate made a doubtful face. Exactly what he thought.

"I'm not hungry anyway." A beat of quiet, and Jacob caught up to himself, realizing he acted as if he was the only person who mattered. "Are you hungry?"

"I'll make a sandwich."

Man, had he always been this self-concerned? There had been a time when all he'd wanted in the world was to see that Kate got what she wanted. That she was happy. A stable life with a nice home and someone who wouldn't take advantage of her the way her mother had.

Now here he was, taking advantage of her.

Jacob sloshed forward until he could peek around Gert's open door. Kate had retreated inside and now sat at the bench, her laptop on her thighs.

"I could walk to a service station and get you something, if you want," he said.

Kate glanced over, mild surprise lifting her brows. Her smiled response was small, but at least it was something. "Not in the budget, remember? We've got plenty of peanut butter. I'm fine."

Jacob nodded. Money. How could he so easily forget that he couldn't just go buy something to make up for his being self-absorbed?

The click-clack of keys let him know Kate had resumed working. Slipping off his wet shoes, he tucked them under the dashboard and stepped up the two risers into the skoolie. "Are you working on a book or the blog?"

"Marketing. For my first series."

Cautiously, he stepped toward her and then lowered onto the narrow bench. "How's that going?"

"Not great." She didn't look up, just continued her search. "Sales aren't where I'd hoped."

Her mouth pulled into a frown. Maybe concentration did that to her, but Jacob wondered if it was more frustration than that. Because of him? Or because sales weren't what she wanted?

"Can I help?" he asked.

Her fingers stilled on the keys, and she turned her chin to meet his eyes. "With marketing?"

"Whatever." Her hesitancy made him feel like he was on the

edge of overstepping. "I won't tell you what to do..."

As she thought, Kate's nose wrinkled and her mouth scrunched sideways in a look that was both adorable and intriguing. "I hate marketing."

"Okay..."

"*You* might not hate it."

Jacob warmed to her softening gaze. "I wouldn't know. I've never done it before."

"I have a couple of online courses I can still access."

Jacob waited, not sure where she was going with that, but thrilling that her blue gaze danced a little. "Were they helpful?"

She turned back to her screen and clicked open a saved link. "Yes, but I still think I'm not getting it. I just don't think analytically."

When she found what she wanted, she looked back at him, and the small thrill in his heart expanded. Jacob held an electrified breath. There, in Kate's eyes, in her increasingly eager smile, was hope. A big, unexpected hope of things to come, better things. And maybe not just for her writing career—something she'd carved out on her own without him even understanding how amazingly capable she was. All at once Jacob felt proud of her, and thrilled for her, and a burgeoning need to do anything she needed him to do to uphold her.

"You think that way though." Kate swiveled the laptop so that Jacob could share the screen with her. "You love analyzing things. I think you could be really good at this."

Breath catching, he cautiously shifted so that he could lay his arm across the back of their small shared bench. Kate wanted him in on this with her! After all the ways he'd failed her, after the disappointments that had made it seem like life and love between them was hopelessly dead, here was this moment.

Such a small thing, to watch a few videos together, to see if maybe he could help with something she didn't like. But it felt like the thawing of spring.

Kate moved to tuck her feet up onto the sliver of bench remaining, her shoulder brushing his chest as she did so. He missed the warmth of her body against him as she settled again. If he curled the arm he'd draped behind her around her instead, would she freeze?

As the introduction to the course played on her screen, he toyed with the possibilities.

There was a lot of hard, emotional things between them still. Maybe one small move at a time would be best.

The first video session only lasted twenty minutes, and after making up his mind to let Kate's actions determine his, Jacob had narrowed his focus onto what was being taught on screen. At some point he'd reached across the space to the drawer where they'd stored a couple of pens and notebooks, retrieved one of each, and jotted down a few notes.

After the conclusion of that video, he tapped the inked line reading *test multiple smaller audiences.* "How did this go?"

Kate looked at what he'd written, then shrugged. "I tested a few. Found one that I thought was working. Then I thought it wasn't, so I shut that down and found out that was a mistake. That's what I was working on—fixing that mistake. Unfortunately, I have several ads targeting that audience, and I'm not sure which one to restart."

"Can I see them?"

She eyed him, and he wasn't sure if that look was because she didn't trust him or if she was embarrassed to show him her efforts.

"You won't lecture me about my lack of organization?"

Ah, so it was the second possibility. "Promise."

She drew a breath as if inhaling courage and nodded. With the finger pad on the laptop, she clicked and typed her way to a marketing platform. "Do you want me to try to explain the mess, or do you want to see if you can figure out the chaos on your own?"

"I'm not familiar with this platform, what everything is, or what I should be looking for."

"The next video helps with that."

"Okay, then would it be better if we watched that first?"

"Probably. But I'm really hungry." Kate transferred her computer to him. "Do you mind if I make a sandwich while you watch it? I've seen it three times."

Jacob watched. Kate ate. She made him a sandwich too.

By the time the second video ended, Jacob had a fresh page of notes, a better idea of how that marketing platform had been designed, and a growing interest in the whole thing. While the past hour of Marketing 101 seemed to have dragged Kate into exhaustion, Jacob felt ramped up about testing images and audiences.

"It's seems a little bit like a game," he said.

"If you say so."

"What's your budget for this?"

She named a number for the month.

"What kind of return have you seen?"

Misery made her expression pinch. "I'm too tired to try to figure it tonight. Numbers give me a headache and make me grumpy."

Maybe that was why she'd been so withdrawn and scowly lately. No, he knew that definitely wasn't it, not entirely at least. He didn't get to let himself off the hook that easily. Closing the laptop, Jacob turned to examine the woman beside him.

"I can do this, Kate. I need to learn the systems, but I can help with it. We...we could be good partners." He finished quietly, almost holding his breath.

For a moment, their gazes held, and with it, a softening. But then... A sheen glazed Kate's blue eyes, and she dropped her look to her hands.

"Kate..." Jacob whispered. Things had been good for the past hour. What had happened? Had he overstepped?

"I'm tired, Jacob. Can we get the skoolie leveled so I can go to bed?"

How foolish it was to think that all the heartache between them could simply evaporate in an hour's time. "Yeah."

Suddenly weary himself, Jacob pushed to stand and then shuffled to the stairs. He slipped his cold, wet shoes back on his feet and pulled a headlamp from the giant glovebox. "Start her up, will you? Hopefully, Gert will pull herself right out of that hole and we can get her squared."

***

Gert did not pull herself out. For the record, Kate had known that particular miracle would not visit them that night.

Standing alongside the skoolie with headlamp in place, Jacob hollered a "Hold up, Kate! She's digging in deeper."

Kate released the pressure she'd held on the gas pedal and looked up at the rearview mirror. The beam of light streaming from her husband's head bounced farther toward the back of the vehicle.

"I'm gonna put my shoulder into it."

Slipping from the captain's seat, Kate hopped to the bottom step and hung out of the doorway. "I don't think that's a great idea. We can just deal with this for one night."

"If this doesn't work, we'll do that. This hole isn't that big though. She just needs a little more oomph."

"But—"

"One try. That's it, Kate. I promise."

This had bad plan written all over it. But the Murphy boys as a lot were the stubborn sort, and Jacob had more than his fair share of that family trait. Was it really worth an argument?

Kate stepped back up to the driver's seat and waited for Jacob's signal.

"Ready?" he yelled.

"Yep."

"Give'er some gas!"

She did. The sound of tires fighting mud and the engine revving was shortly joined by Jacob's animated hollering.

"More!...more!"

Kate gunned it. With a sudden jolt, Gertrude leapt forward, and she had to slam on the brakes. How about that—it worked! Laughing, she smacked the steering wheel, set the brake, and hopped off the seat and out of the bus.

The light beam from Jacob's head cut through the night at a

slanted, upward angle facing the opposite direction. Curious. Kate skipped toward it, ready to congratulate her husband on his tenacity. "It worked!"

The shaft of light turned on her, revealing his position. There was her white-collar man, sprawled out on the ground, and from what she could make out behind the stream of light pointed at her, he was covered head to toe in mud.

"Yeah." Jacob's dry tone shared none of Kate's enthusiasm. "Congratulations."

Kate slid to a stop, nearly losing her balance as she hit a slick spot thanks to Gertrude's trail. "You said more."

"I said *no* more."

Oh dear. Oh boy. "I only heard *more*." So much for hopeful new beginnings. Jacob was clearly angry, which strummed at her own irritation. She'd said this wasn't a great idea. She'd said they could just deal with being stuck in the mud for the night. She'd—

Jacob snorted, pulling Kate back out of her head and away from her building steam. When she looked down at him again, he was looking at himself. And laughing.

The tight ball of tension that had just rolled in her gut unfurled, and in its place moved an uneasiness. Maybe Jacob was losing his mind right before her eyes. "Are...are you okay?"

"Actions and consequences."

The light beam shone in her face again, blinding her from his expression. But rather than anger, amusement filled his tone. "That's what my dad would say to me right now."

"But...are you okay? Is this like a maniacal laugh?"

"Are you asking if I've lost it?"

"Uh...yes."

Jacob's full laugh boomed into the night. "Maybe. Maybe it's about dang time I lose it, right?"

Kate's mind swam with confusion. Jacob didn't laugh at his mistakes—and he definitely did not appreciate it when others did. He most certainly wasn't the kind of man who would sit in a mud hole and crack up about it. But there he was, cracking up.

He rolled toward her and pushed himself out of the muck.

Removing the headlamp so he no longer blinded her, he stood a foot before her, the gentler indirect light revealing his genuine, not-crazy, not-angry smile.

Kate's heart pooled a little. How long had it been since she'd seen that smile? She stared into his eyes, warming as he looked at her.

"What are you gonna do with me, Katie?" he said in a low, almost intimate voice.

An electrical current ran down her spine and over her arms. "Good question," she whispered. Suddenly the gap between them was halved, and she reached to touch the bit of sagging, mud-soaked hair that had fallen near his eye. The amusement in his gaze transferred to something intense and exhilarating, causing her heart rate to surge.

The warm feel of his hand pressed on her hip. Goodness, but it'd been a while since she'd experienced this with him. Kate shivered and Jacob froze. A swirl of questions and long-tamped longings filled the small space between them, and Kate's hand trembled as she lowered it back to her side.

They'd had chemistry from the beginning, but this physical reaction to his nearness, his touch, took her by surprise. In the past few years, it had seemed that the chemistry had run out, replaced by disillusioned resentment. A realization that they'd made a mistake, many of them...

Right then, however, being with this man didn't feel like a mistake.

"I'm a mess." Jacob removed his hand and stepped backward, his gravelly tone revealing more emotion than his words. Fear. Yearning. Disappointment.

Kate heart strummed. "Yes."

His stare was an igniting caress. His heated look traced over her eyes, her cheeks, her mouth, and then her eyes again. She felt her lips part as his head dipped. Her pulse leapt again. But once more, he froze. His chest rose and fell. Rose and fell. And then he pulled away.

"Guess I get to try out the gravity shower tonight."

Kate cleared her throat as hot blood throbbed through her veins. Mud or no, she'd longed for his mouth to touch hers. They were a mess though—a mess that had nothing to do with mud. Maybe she'd been the one to lose her mind.

With a hand to her shoulder and a gentle squeeze, Jacob moved around her. She turned back to follow him. "It'll be freezing. The water hasn't been out in the sun to warm."

He looked back over his shoulder, and she thought she could see a flash of a grin. "My own fault."

Who was this man walking around with her husband's face and an entirely different attitude? All covered in mud and grinning anyway. All pummeled by life, yet gazing at her like *she* made it all better. Goodness, but he was...sexy.

It took twenty minutes to level Gert out and set up the gravity shower off the back end.

The back door hung wide open, and strung between it and the ladder that scaled the frame of the skoolie to the roof, a wire line held a weighted shower curtain. Jacob hefted one of two five-gallon shower bags, filled with clean water, to the outside of the doorframe. He then fastened the small hose to the threaded bottom spout. At the other end of the hose, he attached the water-saving shower head.

Kate tossed a sheet towel onto the far end of their bed, where Jacob could reach it from their "shower," and then busied herself by filling their electric teakettle and plugging it in. That done and set to boil, she stacked slender cuts of pine heartwood into the narrow wood burner. She'd never been good at building fires—usually created more smoke than flame. But Jacob was bound to be halfway to hypothermia by the time he got done. And building an actual fire, rather than smoldering about the man washing himself mere feet away, was a good distraction.

A sharp inhale from the opened back of the bus hit her with confirmation. The water rinsing mud from Jacob's head was cold.

He showered in record time and managed to remove most of the mud while doing it. By the time the setup had been taken down and the skoolie closed tight for the night, Kate's small fire finally took. The pine popped within the small wood burner, offering a meager bit of heat. Dressed in sweats and a thick hoodie, Jacob sipped steaming tea. Grabbing a damp washcloth she'd wet with warm water from the kettle, Kate swiped a few brown splatters from his neck and one large spot from behind his ear.

Tension hummed between them, one of a different variety than what had existed in the recent past. Kate fought against the physical pull, terrified that though the thrill she knew was possible between them might be amazing, the crash could be equally horrendous. She wasn't ready for that risk.

Jacob, it seemed, wasn't ready for it either. After his teacup was empty, he brushed his teeth and climbed into their small bed. Kate quickly followed. Tucked under the blankets and thick quilt, she stared into the darkness, trying to dampen her awareness of the man lying at her side.

He shivered, and she could not ignore it. The very moment she'd made up her mind to roll into him, he shifted to his shoulder, facing her.

"Kate."

"Yeah."

"Can I hold you?"

Yes. I want you to... Why did it feel so dangerous to say? They were married, and this could be a good step toward a better relationship.

"I'm just cold," he said into her silence. The retreat in his words nicked her heart.

She did roll into him then, curving an arm around his trembling frame. He stopped shivering long before she felt the muscles of his back and shoulders relax, and she was tempted to tip her face up to his to see if he'd look at her like he had earlier that night.

To see if he'd finish that dip toward her mouth.

But she didn't. The cowardly part of her won out. Eventually, she slept.

Jacob was gone by the time she woke up.

***

He arrived at five, just as Salazar had instructed. Darkness still held the valley in its grip, but the eastern edge of the skyline whispered of break of day.

Jacob's phone buzzed in his back pocket, and he quickly checked the text as he followed the other hands into the assigned field for the day. Bryce.

Arise, and work! And may the LORD be with you! That's from 1 Chronicles 22—David to his son. Just wanted you to know I'm praying for you, buddy. Remember, work hard, stay humble, and treat everyone like friends and family.

Jacob grunted a laugh into the chilly almost-morning air as he slid his phone back into his pocket. So then. This new life began today. Jacob prayed he'd have the strength to endure and then thanked God for sending Bryce into his life.

It was not lost on him that this was the first morning in a very, very long time in which he'd begun the day in prayer.

Chapter Fifteen
(in which Jacob makes some new friends)

He'd survived two weeks. No, survived wasn't the right word for
it. Maybe it had been, those first few days, but now... Arching
backward, every muscle from the back of Jacob's legs all the way
up to the base of his skull made their protest known. At least he
was walking upright and semi-normal though, unlike the end of
his first day two weeks before. That day...let's just say it had been
good he'd started with prayer, because he'd absolutely needed it.

Jacob had never felt the majority of muscles that had wrenched
in protest that first day. At one point he literally could not move
himself out of a constricted ball of pathetic humanity. By
midmorning, five hours into his first shift as a picker, his entire
back had cramped, dropping him to his knees. A pair of
compassionate co-pickers came to his rescue, rolling him onto the
dirt in between rows of lettuce. They had tugged his body
straight, stretching out his legs and pulling his arms overhead.

"Just breathe, gringo," one of the young men had said, using
the name most of the pickers had tagged him with. Though Jacob
knew it was often used as an insult to men such as himself, the boy
speaking to him said it with a measure of compassion. "Bet you
never even knew you had those muscles back there, did you?"

Chuckling had hurt, but Jacob had done so anyway. "I thought
working for my dad had been hard."

"Made you do a few chores, eh?" The kid pulling his hands—
likely eighteen or nineteen years old—had snickered.

"Yeah. Nothing like this though." Jacob had grunted out his
response through gritted teeth.

"Welcome to a picker's life." A mischievous grin brightened the kids face. "*¡Dichoso!*"

Jacob moaned as his muscles continued to knot hard. "Translate?"

The older one at his feet shrugged, also smiling. "Basically, lucky you, bro."

The trio laughed—Angelo, the one at Jacob's feet (he later found out) and Pete, at his hands—with more enthusiasm than Jacob. The pair had stayed nearby the rest of that first day and throughout his first week. Twice more they had come to his rescue, tugging Jacob's sadly rolled-up body straight again.

When Jacob had arrived before the sun broke earlier this morning, Pete had called "*Buenos días, amigo.*" Friend, not *gringo.*

Though his body still ached and every pore seeped with sweat, Jacob's chest expanded with a feeling that he hadn't experienced often over the past few years he'd spent up in Seattle.

The work had been hard, but the days had been good. He'd gone to bed each night blissfully exhausted and slept like he'd never slept before. He woke with a sense of purpose. After two weeks of this, he sensed a shift in himself, and it felt good.

"Good work today, *Huero.*" Mr. Salazar met Jacob as he exited the east end of the field he'd been working. "Will you show up again in the morning?"

Jacob inhaled a warm breath filled with the smells of warm earth, green goodness, and his own tangy sweat. Bryce had texted him often, sending him encouragement in his easygoing but faithful way. Kate was working hard on both her blog and her newest book, and in the evenings, Jacob would stretch flat on their bed with the laptop on his chest, evaluating ads. It was a quiet, peaceful existence.

"Yes, sir, Señor Salazar." Jacob flashed a smile to the man walking beside him. "Will you let me back in your fields?"

Señor Salazar grunted, his expression, as always, flint. But there was a kindness in his dark eyes, something Jacob hadn't noticed until his third predawn morning at Salazar Farms. Perhaps that was because Salazar hadn't let him see it until then. Before that, his gaze had been laced with suspicion and doubt. Jacob had a few inklings as to why, and truthfully, he couldn't blame the man. If the shoes were swapped, Jacob might well have the same thoughts.

He remembered Bryce's advice: work hard, stay humble, and treat everyone like friends and family. All Jacob could do was put his back into the job. And man, did he.

"You do the work, you can come back. That's the deal, eh?" Señor Salazar stopped at a sorting station under the shade of a large semipermanent awning.

"It's a good deal." Jacob fought the urge to rub his tight muscles. "Thank you."

Salazar looked over the produce being picked through by his employees. The prime fruits went into boxes that would later be loaded onto refrigerated trucks and sent to market. The seconds into other boxes that would be sent to other markets—canneries, mostly. In a rapid cadence of Spanish from which Jacob had no hope of catching any familiar words to try to untangle, Señor Salazar called to a girl across the worktable and then pointed. She responded "Sí" and then turned to scurry to the large building behind them. When she returned, she passed a smaller box across the space.

The box in hand, Salazar turned back to Jacob. "For the week, until payday."

Jacob looked down at the loot. Carrots. Leaf lettuce. Broccoli. Strawberries. Late-season oranges. His stomach summersaulted with joyful anticipation. It was a treasure chest that made his tastebuds water. Suddenly, he found he needed to blink his vision clear before he looked up.

"Thank you."

Salazar nodded. He held Jacob with a focused look for one long moment and then turned away. "Hope to see you in the morning, *Huero*."

Walking toward the dirt-packed road where he'd parked the Grom earlier that morning, Jacob lifted the open box of produce to his face and inhaled. Shutting his eyes, he groaned and then pictured Kate's reaction.

Man, he hoped she'd laugh. Really, truly laugh. And maybe fling her arms around his neck. That'd be incredible.

Maybe this was as good as it got.

At the bike, Jacob set the box on the seat and folded the top flaps closed. Then he carefully secured it to the small back carrier with a few bungees that had been stowed under the seat pad. Satisfied his cargo would be safe, he straddled the bike, kick-started the engine, and took off toward the campground where he and Kate had settled in, about a forty-minute ride from Salazar Farms.

The sun warmed his back and shoulders, its gentle heat working like practiced fingers against the dull ache. As the tension unfurled, Jacob smiled. He guided the Grom down the highway toward home.

Toward Kate.

Yeah. This could be as good as he got. And it wasn't bad. Not bad at all.

***

Kate nibbled on her bottom lip until she heard the moan of the Grom. Looking up from her phone screen, she could make out the slender dust trail that indicated where the bike was. Sighing, she fought against the urge to slide her phone into a drawer and forget the text that had ruined her afternoon.

She and Jacob had been working on being honest, and he'd know her mood was sour—she wasn't as good at hiding her emotions these days. Likely that had to do with their very close living quarters.

The buzz of the bike grew louder, and then suddenly there was her husband, setting the kickstand, pulling off his helmet, and smiling as if he'd won a prize. Goodness it had been so good to see him smile the past week. It was as if he'd been reset, and he was finding the man she'd fallen for again.

She hated to ruin his day. Squeezing the phone, she struggled to know what to do.

"How are you?" Kate opted for a smile as she stood up from her camp chair and strode toward him.

Jacob's smile grew wider. "I bring you gifts, my lady."

At his mirth, Kate felt herself easing toward lightness, and she chuckled. "Do you now? Can we afford such things?"

"No money was exchanged." Jacob unstrapped a box he'd bungeed to the back of the Grom, and then opened it.

Kate stepped forward to peer inside. "Jacob!"

His hand warmed her hip, and when she looked up at him, he grinned down at her. "Produce, the stuff we've been dreaming of. Now the score is even, right?"

Without calculation or reservation, she lifted to her toes and kissed him. The arm around her folded her in against him, and she felt his deep chuckle. For a moment, they stayed that way, and it was beautiful. Then his grip loosened, and he reached to retrieve an orange from the box. Kate accepted the gift, holding it to her nose and inhaling deeply. Bright citrus filled her senses, and she moaned in pleasure.

"What will you do with it?" he asked.

"We're going to eat it." She grinned as she ripped into the peel. "Now."

Again, Jacob laughed, squeezing her shoulders. "You enjoy it. I'm going to shower."

It felt so delightfully ordinary, that exchange. So easy and normal. Could they always be this way, please?

Kate peeled the remainder of the orange, saving the peel to place in a heavy pot full of water to set on the wood burner that night. The sweet scent would permeate their living quarters, adding a touch of joy. Once the fruit was opened and separated, Kate slowly ate each segment, sucking on the juice and savoring the sweetness. In reality, it was not a prime specimen. It was slightly chewy and not as bright as one expected of an orange—most likely because it was nearly out of season, and this would most assuredly be a second. But it was heaven to Kate.

As she finished her half—having determined to keep the other for Jacob no matter what he'd said—Kate sorted through what remained in the box. The greens and orange and red were a feast for her eyes, the aroma a celebration to her sense of smell. She mentally added each item to her menu for the week and felt like the luckiest girl on the planet.

A thought that pushed her mind back to the text that had muddied her mood earlier.

The slight bang of Gert's back doors shutting alerted her to the end of Jacob's shower. He'd become efficient with that—the setup, the teardown, and the quick but effective washing in between. It helped that they left the buckets of water on the roof, taking them down only to refill. That way the water would warm in the unrelenting California sun during the day.

Kate glanced over her shoulder and then turned to meet Jacob at their camp chairs. He lowered into one, and she into the other.

"How was your day?" He rubbed water from his hair and then shook it out.

"Well..."

Jacob stopped midmotion and looked at her. "Something happen?"

"Yes." She retrieved her phone and tapped the screen until the text opened. "This is from my mom."

She watched her husband's jaw tense as he read.

The baron sent another notice on this trailer lot. You got away with this selfishness last month, but we need help. I raised you, Katie-bug. And that don't even count how I've been lying for you to those fancy-pants in-laws. You've been lucky in life, and you owe me. 'Less if you want those Murphys to know all about who you really are.

As he read, Jacob's focus turned into a hard stare, and his mouth flattened into a thin line. His blue gaze was fierce when he turned it to her. "How long has she been doing this?"

"You know she's asked for money almost since the day we got married."

"No, I mean the blackmail. How long has she been blackmailing you, Kate?"

Blood throbbed hot through her veins as a rise of panic and self-defense flooded her. She looked away, feeling the squeeze of a building headache and the tension of an oncoming fight.

Then his hand covered hers.

"Katie." With one soft-spoken breath, Jacob diffused her mounting defensiveness.

Kate exhaled and searched his face again, finding that his eyes still gleamed with fire. But the blaze hadn't been aimed at her. There she'd gone again, believing the worst about him.

"What should I do?" she whispered.

"Nothing. I'll call her."

"She won't talk to you."

"Then I'll text her."

"What will you say?"

"I'll tell her to stop threatening my wife."

"She'll simply threaten you."

At that, Jacob shrugged, a wry grin toying on his lips. "With what? We've already lost everything."

Kate wanted to find comfort in his unexpected amusement, but it seemed he wasn't understanding the situation. "She'll tell your parents, Jacob."

Again, he shrugged and sagged back into his chair. "Probably about time they know, don't you think?"

Shocked, Kate stared at him.

"This lie we've created—it's foolish anyway. Hasn't done us any good. Might be best for everyone if we just tell the truth."

She knew he was right, though her spine wobbled with dread at the thought of it. "That's likely so, but wouldn't it be better if they heard the truth from us?"

At that Jacob paused, scanning the wide-open vastness of desert hills and scattered scrub brush, of bleached boulders the size of small houses in the distance, and interesting Joshua trees poking up like scattered yucca-crested driftwood jammed into the ground. After several moments, he sighed. "Yes. It'd be better if it came straight from us. From me. But that doesn't mean you should cave to your mother's demands."

Kate blinked, usure if the moisture in her eyes was because Jacob was acting as her defender or because she was simply upset at everything all over again. "What should I do?" she repeated.

"Nothing." Jacob handed back her phone and then touched her arm. "Don't respond to her, and we'll see how long that holds."

Kate didn't like it. Mostly, she didn't like that she felt helpless.

ThisBoondockingLife entry #8

> *On the surface, it seems like this would be an*
> *adventure of isolation. After all, we're*
> *avoiding the crowded, expensive*
> *campgrounds. We're living basically off grid.*
> *We're doing life a totally unique way.*
>
> *But it's not done in isolation. Not even close.*
> *Perhaps more than that "normal" way of life,*
> *this boondocking living has revealed to us how*
> *much we truly do depend on people. How very*
> *much we cannot make it entirely on our own.*
> *And this has become a healthy revelation.*
>
> *We have been thrust into the grace and*
> *kindness of others. Perhaps what has been*
> *most surprising thus far is how much we have*
> *not been disappointed in that.*
>
> *There is goodness in this world after all.*

Chapter Sixteen
(in which Kate needs help)

Four days and a camp move later, Kate pried her eyes open and blinked into the bright morning light. Goodness her head hurt. With the bit of energy she could summon, she kicked the blankets and quilt off her body and lay an arm across her forehead.

She felt like she'd been stuck on a moving Tilt-a-Whirl. *God, make it stop!* Groaning, she rolled to her side, and a hard wave of nausea had her squeezing her eyes shut. Oh, no... No...no...no...

She stumbled up the aisle toward the driver's seat and snagged the garbage can sitting under the dashboard. The first heave buckled her legs, and she landed on the wood floor near the steps.

Her stomach emptied violently. Just as it had three times before during the night.

A cold sweat descended over her body when the nausea dissipated. Kate slumped into a fetal position on the floor as a hot tear rolled over her cheek.

Poor Jacob. She really hoped he'd slept a little bit during the night, though she couldn't imagine how he could have, with her puking through half of it.

Goodness, what a disappointment. They'd been doing well, figuring out this boondocking thing over the past three weeks. Finding a new rhythm together, Jacob's softening, her books sales looking better, the produce, even the last camp move they'd made had all been positive. So much so that last night, they'd decided they could celebrate. Dinner in a restaurant...

Just like everything else in her life, the good had swiftly morphed into horrible.

Kate tucked her clammy face into the crook of her arm. "Why this roller coaster, God?"

Pent-up emotions suddenly crashed without enough warning for Kate to build any sort of defense against them. This year—no, this life—there had been so many disappointments. From the time her mother had taken what Kate had earned and saved, it seemed her world had been set on a track of hard lows intermittently broken by glimmers of hopeful promise that only seemed to make the downswings worse.

Falling in love with Jacob had been glorious. Finding that his pursuit of her had been driven by a vindictive jealousy of his younger brother—whom she'd been dating—had been heartbreaking. Being given a home larger and more comfortable than a double-wide had been promising. Discovering that living in an empty house, no matter how lovely, could be just as lonely and cold had been a gut punch. Wealth—or at least the appearance of it—had been about as freeing and fulfilling as a tomb. And the apex of devastation?

Losing the tiny lives that had sprouted in her womb. Sweet little miracles, offering her another hope for fulfillment and love, taken from her body and heart before she could ever hold them in her arms.

Weak and unable to battle the darkness of it all, Kate tucked into a tighter ball right there on the cold wood floor of the skoolie and sobbed. God had turned his back on her long ago, and that wasn't changing.

She should have left Jacob in Seattle—smart man that he was, he would have figured something out. It had been selfishness veiled by faux compassion that had driven her to offer for him to come with her. Secretly—manipulatively, as usual—she'd hoped that his heart would bend toward hers in all this. She hadn't realized that a month ago, but lying there with her heart split wide open, she knew that it was true.

Happiness was not to be had by her, and it was cruel of her to continue to hold on to him.

***

Jacob pulled his hat off by the bill and ran his forearm across his sweaty brow. A glance up at the sky told him there'd be no relief from the building heat of the early afternoon. That wasn't the problem, not what had given him a persistent headache and had anchored a load of unease in his gut.

His mind hadn't left the skoolie all day. An image of Gert, backed up close to a boulder the size equal to the bus, wouldn't budge from his mind. The campground was primitive—offering an outhouse, and that was pretty much it. And it was empty. Kate was there alone.

That lead weight of anxiety sank deeper, burning as it did. Kate was sick. Really sick. He suspected food poisoning, because while she'd been vomiting round the clock, he hadn't felt the slightest bit nauseous. They shared 160 square feet of space—if this had been the stomach flu, it was highly unlikely he'd escape it. Also, she should have been better by now.

His suspicion was further solidified by the fact that the night before she fell ill, they'd gone out to eat. Their once-a-month treat. They'd found a dive they could afford. Kate had gone for alfredo. Jacob had eaten meatloaf. Both had said the food left a lot to be desired, but after two weeks of rice and beans—generously supplemented by the seconds produce Salazar had given Jacob—they were not about to waste food they'd paid real money for.

Kate had started puking about two hours after they'd returned to their newly set up camp at the non-fee national forest site. It'd been three days, and she wasn't getting better. Not only could she not keep anything down, but she'd started mumbling alarming things, almost incoherently, and crying.

Kate wasn't the crying type of woman. Nor was she the type to say the things that she'd been saying. He'd never known her to ride wide swings of emotion the way she'd been the past few days.

You should have left me at the bus stop. Why did you stop? Why did you give me a ride? You could have married anyone else... Jake, why did you choose this life? Was it worth it—just to get back at your brother?

Why did you come with me? You could have found your feet again in Seattle. You shouldn't stay with me...

Jacob looked over his shoulder toward the Santa Rosa Wilderness in the distance. Kate was up there alone, and he was almost an hour away. She needed a doctor, and he was standing there sweating in the middle of a field.

"*Huero.*"

The sharp bark of a man made Jacob nearly jump. Whipping around, he found Señor Salazar striding toward him, a hard frown pressed on his mouth.

"You came to work. Work."

"Yes, sir. Sorry." Jacob shuffled, scanning the row of cauliflower he was supposed to be harvesting. Spotting the place where he'd stopped, he eased back onto the ground. His back still ached, as did his hamstrings, but the pain wasn't close to what it had been that first week. Gripping the sharp knife Pete had lent him, he slid the blade through the base of a ripe head, caught it before it dropped to the ground, and slipped it into the sling bag anchored on across his torso.

"Jacob." This time Salazar not only used his actual name, but his tone came out with less edge.

Looking up, Jacob squinted against the brilliant sun to make out Salazar still standing there. "Sir?"

"Come with me."

Great. Just perfect. Jacob had counted on this job for at least another two weeks. Now, because he'd stared off in the distance, worried about his wife, he was getting fired.

God, are You watching?

Holding the burlap produce bag so that it wouldn't bounce while he walked, damaging the goods, Jacob followed Salazar down the row and toward the central building of the farm. Passing through the doors, the shade of the building offered immediate relief from the heat of the unhindered sun. Adjusting his sight to the darkness within took Jacob a few moments. By the time he had, he found himself in Salazar's office.

"Sit."

Jacob hesitated. Did he need to sit to hear the words *You're fired, Huero?*

"Relax. Your job is safe." Señor Salazar passed a glass of cool water he'd just filled to Jacob and then nodded to the straight-back chair facing his desk. "Something is going on with you. You're distracted. Why?"

Salazar was worried about what was bothering him? Why did he care, other than Jacob wasn't doing his work as well as he should?

"I know a troubled man when I see one," Salazar pressed.

"I've had trouble since I first came to you."

"True. And you were desperate to work, which tells me your trouble might be fixed by employment. It's not fixed though. By the look on your face when you stare at the mountains, I'd say your trouble is worse. I pray to *Dios* every day, and He speaks to me. Here." With a palm, he covered his chest. "I feel you need help."

Warm moisture filled Jacob's eyes, and he blinked. "God told you I need help?"

"*Sí.*"

Overwhelmed, Jacob leaned elbows to knees and dropped his head to his hands. *You do see.* He squeezed his eyes shut as he rolled his fists, fighting to control his rolling emotions. A thick, warm hand covered his shoulder.

"Tell me what is wrong."

"My wife is sick."

"Sick?"

"Yes. She keeps throwing up. Can't keep anything down, and she's been incoherent."

Señor Salazar stepped away, snagged another straight-backed chair, and placed it in front of Jacob. He sat in it. "How long?"

"Three days."

"So she wasn't sick when you first arrived in the valley?"

"No. I think she's got food poisoning." Jacob met Salazar's eyes and found real concern there. "Now she's dehydrated, but I can't afford a hospital bill. I don't know what to do."

"Where is she?"

"Back at the—" Jacob swallowed, looking back at his hands as heat washed over his neck. "At the skoolie, up in the hills."

"Ah. A boondocker."

He nodded, still not looking at Señor Salazar.

"But not by choice," Salazar pressed.

"Something like that."

The room settled into a silence. As the chill of the indoors seeped deeper into Jacob's skin, drying the sweat on his back and nearly making him shiver, Jacob suddenly felt as if he were sitting in front of his father, confessing all his failures. It was a surreal sensation, one that felt equally terrifying and relieving. Though Dad was a firm man with high expectations, he was also a godly man, full of compassion.

Why did Jacob continue to hide from such a father? The inkling of answers to that question wove uncomfortably into his heart, but Jacob set them aside, glad when Señor Salazar leaned forward again, touching his shoulder.

"Can you get her down here?"

"My wife?"

Salazar nodded.

"The road is pretty rough for about eleven miles, and I don't think she can ride the Grom right now. I'd hate to move the skoolie only to have to go back up that same bumpy road later, and the only places to park overnight near here are loud and not very private. Not safe."

Again, his boss nodded. "I have a place for you to park, near my home. And my wife is a nurse practitioner."

Jacob's head jerked up. "A nurse practitioner?"

A proud, if not knowing, grin tipped Salazar's mouth. "Surprised?"

Lowering his gaze to the floor, Jacob nodded. "I guess so." He had no reason to be, and he wasn't exactly sure what that said about him. Certainly not anything good. "You'll help us? You both will?"

"*Dios* says to do unto others as you would have done to you." Salazar's low chuckle released the lingering tension in Jacob's chest. "Even to those who live in a bus, *Huero*."

Jacob rolled one hand into the other and squeezed. "You continue to give me kindness, and I know you didn't have to in the first place. There are plenty of other people..." A swelling lump cut off his words. He cleared his throat and stood. "I'll go finish that row."

"Go get your wife."

"I still have an hour left on my shift."

"Bring your wife down from the mountain. Then we'll see about work."

Thisboondockinglife entry #10

> *There are things you don't plan for.*
>
> *The beauty of that life fact as a boondocker is that you are suddenly thrust into a position of need, and you discover that there are people with amazing hearts. Experiencing this wonder hidden within the many challenges life can throw at you makes you want to be a better person. Maybe that's the way it was supposed to be all along.*
>
> *We are learning not just a new way of life, Jake and me. We are learning a new way of thinking—and of being.*

Chapter Seventeen
(in which Kate makes a new friend)

Why did she still feel so awful?

Mind blurred, Kate rolled onto her side and pried her eyes open. The container Jacob had appointed as her sick bucket sat at the ready. As another nauseating cramp twisted her stomach, Kate groaned. Three days ago, she'd been sure she would be done with this. A twenty-four-hour bug shouldn't last this long.

A shiver trembled over her as the interior of Gertrude lacked the warmth of a fire, and she gathered the blankets closer. Thank heavens, the nausea subsided—no throwing up this round. Still, she felt like she'd been beat with a baseball bat.

"God, help."

This wasn't how this was supposed to go. She'd lost days of writing, setting her schedule back so far that the loss, at this point, was unrecoverable. Added to that, she'd not peeked at her marketing efforts in nearly a week. Heaven knew what her spend was. Half of her ads had been test runs that she'd set up while Jacob had been at work, and she hadn't gone over them with him. The really bad news was that test runs rarely proved out as successes. That meant they'd been left running unwatched, spending her meager resources like she was a rich woman without a care.

She had a whopper of a care. They could be in a whole lot of trouble.

A flush of heat washed from her scalp and down her entire frame, bringing with it a tight pain in her head. Moaning, Kate held her head between her hands and let the tears roll. She should at least sit up, reach for her laptop, and stop the money bleed that was sure to be happening online. But at her weak attempt, the painful rubber band around her brain tightened, and her empty stomach rolled.

"God..." Her whispered cry went unfinished, leaving her in a black misery. A whirling buzzed in her ears, and Kate willed herself to slip back into sleep. At least there she couldn't think about how awful everything was.

Sleep. Sleep... *Sleep.*

"Katie."

Her name came softly into the hot darkness. Now she was hearing things...

"Katie." This time a cool hand to her forehead accompanied the gentle voice.

Oblivious to how long she'd escaped her misery, Kate cracked an eye open. Jarring sunlight sliced into her vision, broken by a shadowy image of her husband. "Jake?"

"Yeah."

That sunlight was too bright to be evening, too direct to be lowering beyond the hills where Jacob had last parked Gertrude. "What are you doing back here?" Dread filled her as she asked. The plan had been to use his earnings to pay back what he'd owed his contractors. Now, with her being sick and very likely losing money by the moment, they likely needed whatever he could bring in to eat.

So many setbacks. How many more life blows could they handle?

"It's okay." His weight pressed into the thin foam mattress near her hip. "Señor Salazar sent me back."

"You're fired?"

"No. He was worried about you. His wife is a nurse practitioner."

"What?"

"He says to bring you down. They'll help us."

Who was a nurse? What was happening? Nothing about this conversation made sense. How did anyone even know they needed help? Jacob was a proud man—it wasn't likely that he'd told anyone about any part of their dire situation, beginning with they lived in a converted bus and ending with Kate hadn't been able to keep anything down in more than three days. Her husband wouldn't tell people that.

Maybe she'd slipped into full delusion. Wishful thinking taking on hallucination levels. "Jake..." She reached for the hand that had smoothed away her hair. It wasn't there. Had that been real? Likely not—

A dry and calloused palm gripped her fingers. Not the feel of Jacob's hand. At least, not what his grip had felt months before.

Another set of knuckles pressed lightly against her cheek. "You're still pretty sallow."

That was his voice though. Low and laced with concern, but Jacob's nonetheless.

"It's at least an hour drive down the hills, and the first bit of that will be rough. Can you endure it?"

Maybe he was really there? "Who said they would help us?"

"Señor Salazar said his wife would check you to see why you're not getting better."

"Salazar...the farm owner?" Kate fought through the foggy ache in her head as a crack of hope broke through her despair.

"Yes."

"Why?"

"He was worried."

"You told him?" Her heart lifted at the idea. Jacob would have to be really concerned about her to do such a thing.

"Yes. He called me into his office because...because I wasn't working as hard as I had been. I thought he was going to fire me."

"He didn't?"

"No. He wanted to know what was going on."

"Why weren't you working as hard?"

A single finger slid along her temple at her hairline. "I was worried about you. Kept looking toward the Santa Rosas, willing you to get well."

His touch made her dizzy. Or maybe she was just dizzy? For a moment, it was a good kind. Kate moved her chin and blinked until the man leaning over her came into focus. Same handsome face, more prone to serious contemplation than to laughing. Same intense blue eyes, usually sharp and distant, now soft and worried. A rush of something sweetly painful clutched her chest, stealing her breath. Unable to process either thoughts or emotions, Kate pulled the hand that still held hers until she could tuck it against her face. *Please let this be real...* She shut her eyes again, barely stopping the leak of warm tears.

His grip squeezed. "Can you endure for an hour?" he whispered.

"Yes."

He leaned nearer, hovering over her and making her think that he'd press a kiss to her forehead. Making her, in her foggy mental state, wish desperately that he would.

His hand slipped from her cheek, leaving both her face and her fingers bereft of his touch. And then the weight near her hip lifted. As the bus engine growled to life, Kate tucked her face back into the folds of the quilt and swallowed against the knot in her throat.

By the jolting of her home, she determined this was in fact reality. Her heart split wider, filling her with sharp pain. Jacob was there, taking care of her again. The question that had driven painfully into her heart was *why?*

She knew what she wanted that answer to be.

***

"I believe the worst would be past, except your wife is severely dehydrated. That can be fatal." Anitra Salazar's dark eyes settled on Jacob with a grim hold. "How long has it been since she could keep anything down?"

Jacob looked at the dirt under his feet, placing a hand against Gertrude's metal side. Anitra Salazar, APRN, had spent the past fifteen minutes inside the skoolie with Kate. Jacob had waited outside, pacing the small cove beneath a group of palms where Mr. Salazar had directed him to park.

"She got sick four nights ago. It came on kind of sudden. We thought it was a stomach bug, but then she didn't get better."

"What have you given her?"

"Pepto. Water." Jacob shrugged. "Not that any of it stayed down."

Mrs. Salazar nodded. "She says she didn't throw up today."

A thread of relief wove into Jacob's massive worry. "That's good. I didn't know. I was here most of it."

"She also says there's no chance of being pregnant."

Jacob drew in a long breath and looked toward the bus. Something hard pressed in his chest as flames fingered his neck. "No." Was he required to expound on that? That he and his wife weren't currently...sympatico?

He felt her stare on him and forced his eyes to meet hers.

"I'm having her take a test anyway. To be sure."

Great. And if Kate was pregnant? Jacob's legs wobbled, and the world tilted, as if he'd just been whacked on the back of the head. "Okay." What else could he say?

"If she's not, then we can try treatment here. We'll focus on getting her rehydrated, unless I see signs of systems shutting down."

"Why was she so sick?"

"My guess—food poisoning."

Jacob nodded. He'd thought that too.

"Will she be okay?"

The woman's frown eased, and she reached to touch Jacob's

arm. "If she hasn't thrown up today, that's a positive sign. If she is pregnant though, I want her to go to the hospital."

She's not pregnant. Jacob bit back the words and nodded. Though relieved that most likely they wouldn't have to go to a hospital—because how on earth was he going to pay for that?—a vice clamped in his chest. If circumstances were different, he'd be thrilled if she was expecting. Scared, especially because of their painful losses in the past three years, but thrilled.

But unless Kate had something she needed to confess, she *wasn't* pregnant. Jacob was certain.

Without permission, his thoughts moved toward Jackson. His brother was a dad now, and though his marriage to Mackenzie seemed rushed and suspect, by the group pictures Jackson sent out of himself, Mackenzie, and little Bobbie Joy, Jackson had landed on his feet, laughing. As usual.

At the burn of resentment, Jacob rubbed his chest. Did he really want anything different for Jackson?

No. Not truly. It was just that Jacob couldn't help but feel that for all of Jackson's triumphs, Jacob was the recipient of failure. Everything always worked out for Jackson, and people liked him. Things had a way of going south for Jacob—and he wasn't that popular with anyone.

Except Connor and Kate. Well, at one point, Kate.

Why was he so broken?

"Mr. Murphy?"

Jacob looked up, suddenly aware that he'd stared off toward the northern mountain range, as if he'd been alone. "I'm sorry. Could you say that again?"

Mrs. Salazar studied him with empathy and then squeezed his arm again. "I'll go now, but I'll be back. We'll take care of you and your wife, Mr. Murphy."

As she walked away, Jacob slipped into a deep well of unworthiness. The Salazars had no incentive to take care of them. And there he'd been, sulking.

Might be a reason his life seemed so hard, reasons that had nothing whatsoever to do with Jackson or any of his other brothers. Maybe it didn't have to stay that way.

One of the many conversations he'd had with Bryce repeated in his mind. Bryce had handed him a small copy of *Our Daily Bread*. Jacob had looked at it, wondering at the randomness.

"I see you staring at my Bible in the mornings."

Not so random then. "Yeah," Jacob had said. "Makes me think of my dad. He does that too—reads his Bible every morning."

"So you've said." Bryce raised a brow. "But not you."

He'd shrugged. "Never got into it, I guess."

"Jacob, I'm not one to tell another man what to do. Your life is your life, bro. But I am one to say what I think, as a neighbor and a friend. Here's the truth. I think you've been lost a lot longer than since whatever happened up there in Seattle happened. And I'm a real believer in God's ability to take away things that we put in His place—and He does it for our own good. So we stop being lost."

Jacob had frowned, holding up the small paperback volume.

"His Word is a lamp unto our feet and a light unto our path. You wanna stop wandering around in the dark? Bro, you gotta put on the light."

Jacob waved the flimsy book in the air. "This isn't the Bible."

"No, it's not. But used correctly, it'll put you into the Bible." Bryce clapped his back. "It's a place to start, Jacob. So start."

Jacob hadn't felt like arguing, particularly since something deep inside had latched on to the idea. However, when he'd wandered back to the skoolie that morning before he and Bryce had climbed onto the roof for the day, he'd tucked the copy of the daily devotional into his Bible—the first time he'd cracked open the cover in who knows how long—and then stowed them both in the glove box.

Hadn't thought of it since.

Until now.

Jacob pushed open Gert's door and climbed up the steps. Glancing toward the back of the skoolie, he found Kate sitting upright, her legs over the edge of the bed.

"Look at you. Alive." He stepped toward her.

She looked up, her pale face thin and a bluish hue under her eyes. Even as alarm sank through him, she lifted a small smile. "I'm alive," she whispered. Her gaze moved from him to something beside her.

A look was all he needed to know what it was. At one point they'd had a collection of pregnancy tests. He looked back at her, and she shook her head.

Of course she wasn't pregnant. He couldn't read her reaction though. Sad? Hard to be sad when they hadn't even been trying, right? Anyway, at this point a negative was good news.

He kept telling himself that, ignoring his own unreasonable disappointment. Leaning against the small closet a foot from where she slumped, Jacob reached to finger her tangled hair. "Nurse Salazar says she'll get you better."

She nodded. "That would be good." Exhaustion coated her quiet voice. But maybe something more. Despair?

He'd seen her fall into misery before. Every time the tests had come back negative when they'd been trying for a baby. And the times they'd lost the little ones they'd both wanted so much. Kate had slipped into dark depths beyond his reach, and Jacob had felt helpless and insufficient.

Life had not been what either of them hoped for. It hadn't looked anything like what he'd promised her.

Sliding against the wood door of the closet, Jacob crouched in front of Kate. Uncertain his touch would be welcome, he reached anyway, covering her knee. Her chin jerked up, her look jumping to his face in surprise.

"I wish I could make all of this stop."

As a sheen glazed her eyes, her look softened on him. "It's not your fault I got sick."

"This life—" Sudden emotion cut off his words. He inhaled, stabilizing his voice. "It's not what you wanted."

"Seems like we've talked about this before." Timidly, she covered his fingers. "It's what we have."

Unable to look at her anymore, he stared at the floor and nodded.

"Jacob, we have another issue."

More? *Lord, what now?* "Okay..."

"I'm really behind on my word count, and I don't think I'll be able to release on schedule. Also..." She drew in a long breath. "My ads have been running unattended while I've been sick. There's a really good chance I lost money. A lot of it."

Tension unfurled from his shoulders, and Jacob lifted his chin. "No, you didn't."

"What?"

"I've been monitoring them. While you were sick. I watched the rest of those tutorials, and I've been tracking your ads. Tweaked a few of them, turned a couple off. You're not losing money. You're actually doing okay."

Kate held him with a look Jacob hadn't seen in what felt like forever. Gratitude and relief. Her fingers curled around his, and then she sighed.

"Thank you," she breathed, eyes falling shut. She lay down, curling onto her side. "Thank you."

There it was again—a tiny glimmer of hope. For her, for him. For them. And for this life. *Thank You...*

As he lifted that small prayer of gratitude, he remembered what he'd been after. His Bible.

Jacob stood, reached for the quilt that had been thrown to the side, and covered Kate. Then he turned and moved back to the front of the skoolie to open the wide glove box.

There it was, right where he'd left it.

Bryce was right. It was time to stop wandering around in the dark.

ThisBoondockingLife entry #15

>New skills take practice. We realize this
>when we're trying something like, say,
>painting. Or, in my case, writing. There's
>craft to those things, and we realize that
>learning is in the doing, and doing makes us
>better, and so we keep at it. Practice.

>Life though? I don't think we approach life
>like that. We expect everything to just...work.
>And freak out, wail, and then give up when
>they don't. You know, "Tried that. Didn't
>work. Can't be done!"

>Jake and I can't do that as boondockers.
>Why? Because out here, if we give up, if we
>refuse to practice these new skills, we've got
>nowhere else to go. Take, for example, my
>cooking skills. For the record, I started with
>nothing.

>Here's the score:

>Dinners of enjoyable quality prepared by me
>in my skoolie-sized kitchen: almost 1. That's
>right, almost. It would have been a solid 1,
>except I forgot that the dutch oven stays hot
>long after heat has been removed. The bottom
>of our rice and broccoli dish ended up crusty.
>Jake ate it anyway—because he was hungry,
>and working as a harvester demands fuel.

>Dinner fails (of the sort of quality that you
>choke down because you need sustenance):
>every other one since we started this
>adventure four weeks ago. How many is that?
>You can math it if you want—I've no desire
>to. All I need to know is that so far, I'm not
>winning on this.

>But here's the deal—I'm trying again tonight
>because this crazy boondocking couple must

*eat. Going for takeout isn't a financial option
(it isn't practical either). So back to the dutch
oven I'll go. Hopefully, I'll remember to not
get distracted (this is not the time to write an
intense scene for my next novel), to add
enough water to the rice, to flavor the raw
food with salt, and that the dutch oven cooks
hot and long.*

*Practice makes...better. (Perfect ceased to be
the goal around about dinner fail #5. Pro-tip:
realism is part of this boondocking life.)
Here's hoping I can feed my husband
something that he doesn't have to choke down.*

*I'll let you know how the rice and beans turn
out.*

Chapter Eighteen
(in which light glimmers)

"The rice and beans weren't bad, Katie." From his spot on the
sofa bench, the light from Kate's laptop glowing against the gray
dusk, Jacob looked at Kate.

She met his blue gaze, and a twirl of something distantly
familiar swam through her middle. There was something in his
eyes, something wonderful. It was the same something that she'd
seen years back, when he'd take her home to the trailer park. The
way he'd looked at her then, like she was the treasure he'd hunted
for. The one he was determined to claim.

Jackson had never looked at her quite like that. He'd always
had admiration for her, but this deep throbbing *something* had
come from Jacob alone. And it was there again, in his silent study.

Pressing a hand to her belly, she leaned back against the

narrow counter where she'd been cutting the raw vegetables Señor
Salazar had given Jacob that day. She would sort them into
stackable containers to place in their dorm-sized refrigerator—
the supply for the week.

With a lifted heart, Kate shrugged. "Nothing I make will ever
compare to Anitra's food. Or even Sally's, for that matter."

As she thought of the intervention they'd been given over the
past week, gratitude swelled with that warm feeling Jacob's look
had just ignited. Kate felt so much better. Anitra Salazar had
taken such intently good care of her—of both of them—
bringing home brewed broth, electrolyte-supplemented water,
and a box of late-season oranges. For several days, Anitra had
stopped in at the skoolie to check on Kate before she left for her
clinical shift, and then again after. Both she and Señor Salazar
came in the evenings, bringing amazing meals wrapped in foil.
Kate hadn't been able to eat much of those the first couple of
days, but as she regained strength, recovering from the food
poisoning and resulting severe dehydration, she began living like
a functioning human again. When she could eat real food, Kate
reveled in the authentic Mexican dishes.

"We're surviving," Jacob said.

Yes, they were. Thanks to some massive and unwarranted
generosity. The Salazars had rescued them, their acts of kindness
settling deeply in Kate's heart and shifting her view of life and
people a little bit more. Similar to the way Bryce and Sally's
kindness had done.

Jacob shifted, making space on the narrow seating where he'd
been working on Kate's laptop. "You want to sit?"

Her heart fluttered like it had when she'd been eighteen and
he'd offered her a ride home for the second time. Back then, she
probably should have had the sense to know that she needed to
end things with Jackson, because she'd never had this sort of
thrilling reaction with him. Unfortunately, she'd lacked that
good notion.

No, she hadn't lacked it. She'd thought about it and pushed the
conviction away, telling herself Jacob had no real interest in her.

Why would he? Older and going places with all his intelligent potential—why would Jacob be interested in a trailer mouse like her? Telling herself Jackson was her best shot of a life outside of the trailer park, Kate had held on to him until it'd been too late to break things off cleanly.

The shame was on her. Still.

As she lowered next to Jacob, she closed the door against those memories. They made her feel small and ugly, and they also would lead her straight back into the tangled mess that not only existed between her and her now brother-in-law (not to mention her mother-in-law, who had not been very happy with either Kate or Jacob when all was said and done), but more pertinent to that moment, into the chaos that proved to be the shaky foundation for her marriage to Jacob.

If she had known how deeply her manipulative deceptions would reach into her married life, she would have made different choices. If only she'd known...

Shutting off the intrusive thoughts, Kate leaned to peek at the screen facing Jacob. "I thought you were working on marketing."

This new partnership of theirs was working. Jacob had been modest when he'd told her that he'd "tweaked" a few of her ads and that they "weren't losing money." What he'd done seemed to Kate to be a little bit of magic. Sales had doubled in the weeks since Jacob had taken over her marketing department.

Business partners. Keep that up front, Kate spoke to her heart. She and Jacob hadn't worked well as a married couple, and she still couldn't untangle that mess. Perhaps they never would. But they worked as business partners. Jacob's analytical mind and strange delight with data mining perfectly complemented her creative work. Together, her publishing ventures were climbing in the right direction, at a pace she hadn't believed possible.

"I was going to see if I could boost the SEO on your blog, but I got caught up reading your entries." Jacob's chin turned, and again his attention squared on her. "Kate, you're amazingly talented. What you choose to write, your way with story, so perfectly paired with the images you pick to upload—this is captivating."

Biting her lip as a wonderful warmth filled her cheeks, Kate soaked in his serious admiration. Not very businesslike of her at all. "Thank you."

"Why didn't I know?"

She shrugged. He'd been too busy, too consumed with his work.

As if she'd answered him out loud, regret filled his eyes. "I'm sorry I didn't. I should have."

Business partners...

Tentatively, one of Jacob's hands left the keyboard and raised toward her face. When his fingers met her jawline, it was with a feather-soft touch that tingled. Kate's eyes slid shut at the heady sensation, the business-partner mantra fading into silence. Jacob shifted, angling toward her. His thumb traced along her chin, and then his palm slid against her neck. Kate's heart throbbed as he leaned near, his breath warm against her cheek.

"I should have paid attention, Katie." His lips, warm and gentle, pressed near her ear.

Oh goodness...she remembered this. Kate gripped his shoulder as his nose drifted against her face. His lips grazed hers, and her heart throbbed. With his thumb, he tilted her chin and then fitted his mouth to hers. His kiss was tentative and yet full of longing. Kate didn't pull away.

Her laptop set aside, Jacob's arms closed around her as his kisses deepened, mouth exploring hers with growing fervency. She responded, her own desire for him swelling over the dam of suppression constructed of hurt and resentment. Breathless and nearly lost in the euphoria of being wanted, Kate pressed into her husband.

Until one thought crashed through her mind. *I can't lose any more.* No more of her heart. Not to Jacob, not to this failing marriage, and especially not to the agony of yet another miscarried child.

What they had right now was working. And what they had was a business partnership. Not...

She froze. Folded against him, Kate pulled her mouth from his.

She felt the drumming of his heart against her palms as Jacob stiffened. His breath fanned against her face. "Katie..."

Moving back, she let her hands fall away. "We...I can't."

His stare felt heavy, the weight of his disappointment—or perhaps defeat—even more so. "Do you hate me?"

"No, Jake." She blinked, willing herself to look up at him. "Just don't want me anymore."

Clearly she still wanted him—how could he have missed her desire? Shaking her head, she searched for the courage to say what had really happened. That the risk was too great, her heart couldn't take another beating. He wouldn't get it though, and in that her resentment resurrected. Among all the other disappointments between them, Kate had carried the grief of her miscarriages silently. Alone. Jacob had known about them, but rather than being her comfort or even her partner in the grief, he'd gone to work. Just...went to work, went on with life.

He wouldn't understand how deeply scarred those miscarriages had left her. How terrified she was to go through it yet again. And that didn't even address the many other difficulties that defined them as a couple. They'd tried intertwining their lives, their hearts. It failed.

They were better off as business partners.

"I can't go back," she whispered. He could take that however he would. Kate wasn't going to clarify it.

Jacob blew out a long, controlled breath, sitting back as he did. After an extended moment of hard, unreadable silence, he slid away from her. "Okay."

Peeking at him, she looked for his censure. It wasn't there. "Okay?"

"Yeah." He cleared his throat and moved to retrieve the laptop he'd set aside. "I've got some work to do anyway. This blog of yours should go viral." With a flash of a forced smile that didn't ease the tightness around his eyes, he refocused on what he'd been doing before.

Back to work.

Guilt filled the place where resentment had just resided. And frustration. Sally had advised to make the best of this situation. To *choose* happy.

Instead, she'd chosen resentment and fear, to hang on to the hurts and anger from the past. Thing was, Kate didn't know how else to survive.

***

Jacob scowled at his cell as it buzzed against his palm. Why on earth would Jackson call him? Phone conversations with most of his brothers were rare. Calls from Jackson were nonexistent.

Maybe he'd dialed the wrong brother?

Didn't matter. Jacob wasn't going to answer. He was working—and the Salazars deserved a full, focused shift out of him. Personal phone calls didn't figure into that. Pocketing his cell, Jacob went back to picking, careful to pop the strawberries cleanly at the stem without damaging the fruit or the plant. The warm sun would beat down on him from the cloudless blue sky for another two hours before he finished his work. In that time, he hadn't been able to kill the curiosity that Jackson's call had provoked.

Gertrude was still parked beneath the shade of a stand of palms on Salazar land. Señor Salazar had told him to stay put. As Jacob stepped beneath the protection from the sun, he caught a glimpse of Kate. Sitting on a folding lawn chair, she typed away on her laptop, likely trying to make up for lost word counts. He wondered what was happening in the story she was creating. Was the hero wooing his lady with all the right things? Likely. He was probably sweeping the girl off her feet, rescuing her from all of life's disappointments and giving her the perfect life she'd only ever dreamed of.

He was not that man. Nothing could have reminded him more clearly, or more painfully, than Kate's rejection the other night. Jacob paused his steps as that wound throbbed, taking a moment to wrap up the ache and set it to the side. Man, but it hurt though.

Rubbing his chest, he blew out a slow breath and reminded himself that no matter what else there was between him and Kate, they needed each other to survive right then. He continued toward the skoolie he called home.

At the sound of his footfalls, Kate looked up. "Hey."

"Hi."

"How was picking?"

"Hot."

Squinting, Kate looked up. "I'll bet it was, under that sun." She got up. "Want to sit?"

"Nah." What he wanted was to stand under the stream of lukewarm water at the back of the skoolie and hope that his disintegrating mood would trickle away along with the grimy sweat that covered him. But setting up their makeshift shower felt like too much effort at the moment. He motioned toward Gertrude. "I'll just grab some water."

"It's pretty warm in there." Kate set her laptop on the chair and strode across the space of dirt between the trees and the skoolie. She snagged the folded chair that had been leaning next to Gert and took it back to where she'd set up hers. "I'll just put this here, in case."

She was acting out of guilt. He didn't want her guilt-driven kindness.

Jacob nodded but continued into the bus. Kate frustrated him. Their relationship had softened—she had softened toward him. One minute he thought she was really making an effort to make things between them work, and though he knew he'd failed her on an epic scale, he'd allowed himself to think that perhaps they still could. But then she'd pull away from him.

He'd relived that passionate kiss more times than he'd care to admit, and each time he'd tried to understand what had happened, where he went wrong. Had he only imagined their mutual desire? Didn't seem likely—his imagination wasn't anything like hers. But he must have done something wrong.

With a low growl, he opened the small fridge and snagged the reusable water bottle from the door. Why he tortured himself, he had no idea. This life was hard enough.

Then there was that phone call from Jackson. What the heck? Mood growing darker, Jacob capped the water and slipped his cell from his back pocket. With a couple taps on the screen, he had accessed his voicemail box.

"Hey." Jackson sounded anything but like his confident, always-making-fun-of-something self. He cleared his throat. "Hey, Jacob. It's Jack. Don't fall over or anything. Or panic. There's nothing wrong or anything. Well, maybe. The thing is, this is old, don't you think? I mean, we're both grown men now. And we're brothers, right?" Another pause lengthened. "This is maybe not making any sense. Sorry, man. The reason I called was that I was hoping you and Kate were planning on going to Mom and Dad's in May. You haven't met my daughter yet, and, well, it'd be good to see you."

Jacob pulled the cell from his ear and stared at it. He didn't move, maybe even didn't breathe, just stared.

Had that been another one of Jackson's pranks? What was the punch line? If Jacob hated anything, it was to be the punch line.

But it didn't sound like—

To hear the message again, press... the automated voice of his mailbox jarred him back into reality. He jabbed End. What would he do with that? Raising his eyes, he caught sight of Kate as she stared up at the palms above her in thought.

What would she think?

Grabbing the capped water bottle, Jacob strode back down the aisle and steps and then toward his wife.

Her attention moved toward him as he lowered onto the chair she'd set up. "Changed your mind, huh?"

"Yeah."

"It feels so warm, and it's not even May yet. Might be you'll be glad to be done working as a picker after the end of the month."

"Could be." He'd miss Angelo and Pete and the Salazars though. But those thoughts barely registered with him. Instead he squared a look on Kate, took a deep breath, and waved his phone in the air. "Jackson called. Left a message."

"Jackson?" Her brows folded inward.

"Yeah. Crazy, right?"

"Uh, unexpected, yes. Is there a problem?"

"No." He flipped the phone so he could see the screen and brought up voicemail again. Once there, he put it on speaker.

Kate leaned forward, listening. Every word sounded absurd to Jacob, even hearing the whole thing for the second time. What had brought this on? Had Mom coerced Jackson into this? Didn't seem like Mom's style—she wasn't the coercing type. Then again, Jackson wasn't the call-to-make-up-with-Jacob type either.

"Wow." Kate's voice was all wonder, and her eyes were wide when Jacob looked at her.

"Yeah. Something like that." He uncapped the water and tipped back a cool swig. "What do you make of it?"

Kate leaned back in her chair. "You're brothers. He's tired of all of this? Wants to give a shot at being brothers again?"

"We were never close in the first place."

"There's a first time for everything."

"Not everything."

"So you don't want a shot at being brothers?"

Jacob sighed, leaning forward to put elbows to knees. That wasn't it, really. He did want a shot. Thing was... He peeked at Kate, reeling against the feeling of being overexposed. Which was stupid. This woman had seen every horrible aspect of who Jacob Murphy really was. Trying to hide it, to deny that he had any personal issues he didn't deal well with, had only created distance between them.

Then again, she'd rejected him. *Ugh. Man up, Murphy. She's still your wife.*

"That's not it," he said. "Thing is, Kate, I don't know how to be Jackson's brother. Honestly, I'm not good at being much of anything to anyone." Once again daring eye contact with her, he set the truth of it free on a steady, matter-of-fact voice. "A fact that is the major contributor to this gigantic trench between you and me. I'm not good at relationships, and I don't know how to fix that."

***

Every reservation about being authentic with him crumbled. Even if they were better at being business partners than being a married couple, this moment where Jacob entrusted her with the brokenness of his soul—even if it had been done in a chilled and businesslike tone—demanded an honest response from her heart. She had no illusions that such a raw and honest statement hadn't cost him. She knew him too well.

Kate slid from the folding chair, setting aside her laptop, and planted her knees on the ground at his feet. At her approach, Jacob's chin fell toward his chest, and his shoulders jolted. There was the truth. No, that admission hadn't been cheap at all. It had come from the depths of his heart, a lonely place he safeguarded all of his hidden wounds. Both of his hands squeezed his phone, and Kate enclosed them with hers.

"Jake..."

He shook his head, unwilling to look at her, and sniffed. "I thought it would be different with you. That I would be better somehow. Less selfish, less cold. With everything in me, Kate, I swear, that's what I wanted. I just can't seem to find my way from here to there."

Kate pushed into the space where his shoulders curled inward, moving her palms up his chest and over his shoulders, and then wrapping her arms around his neck. Suddenly his embrace surrounded her, taking her in, holding her close. She felt every tremor of his silent cries, and as her own tears leaked, she buried into his neck. He was warm and smelled of sweat, of earth and sun, of hard work, and of the man she remembered falling for.

Maybe this was the way from here to there, to where they both wanted to be. Maybe if he entrusted her with the broken places of his heart, and she gave him hers, they could find their way to the same side of that canyon. A way to be so much more than distant business partners. A way to be truly together in this life.

To get there, though, she'd have to be every bit as bravely honest as Jacob had just been.

Laying her head against his shoulder, Kate summoned her own confessions. "I realized over the past weeks that I made you into my prince charming." She braced her palm against his chest as his hold on her loosened. "I wanted so much for you to be my salvation. My deliverance from the trailer park and everything there that I thought was the root of all my misery."

"I wish I was that man, Katie." He gripped her shoulders. "I wanted so much to be that man."

Kate sat back and found his teary blue gaze. "I think about those fairy tales—and about the stories I write. We assume those characters have a happily ever after. But we never see it, you know? We just think that the high romance—the way Prince Charming and Cinderella felt in that moment at the dance—that's how they'll feel every day for the rest of their lives. And we want that to be true, for them and for us."

His hand covered hers, still on his chest, as his gaze fell to the ground. "I'm so sorry that it wasn't for us. I wanted that too, you know? I wanted all of it. Honest."

"How could it be true for anyone? That's not life. It just can't be, because you and me and everyone else on the planet are messed up." Kate wiped her eyes. "I'm not digging around for an apology from you, Jake, so please don't think that. I'm saying *I'm* sorry. That was a lot of pressure on you. For me to expect that you would save me from everything that made me unhappy, that you'll always be my source of happiness and contentment? I'm realizing how big that is, how unfair that kind of expectation is. And the truth is, I'm responsible for my own happiness. *I* choose how I handle life, how I respond. I can be miserable, or I can make the best of things—just like Sally said."

Jacob broke again, gripping her shoulders. "I wanted to be that guy for you though. I wanted to make you happy. Truly, Katie, I did."

Cupping his cheek, she caught a tear against his nose with her thumb. "But you can't. Any more than I could be your source of significance. We just can't fill those huge holes for each other. It seems like expecting that of each other has torn us apart."

He swallowed, his brow knit deeply with ache and regret. A hint of fear laced his tone as he said, "What are you saying?"

"I'm sorry, Jacob. I'm so sorry that I put expectations on you that belong to God and that I held you accountable for things that ultimately are my responsibility. I'm sorry that I made you feel like so much a failure. You're not."

He shook his head. "I did fail. At a lot of things, including us, I failed."

A hard, hard thing for a proud man to say.

With a quick swipe of his palm, Jacob smudged at the tears on his face. "I've been reading while you write—the Bible like Bryce suggested, and some other things—and I came across something that has been sticking with me. It said that failure can be an excellent teacher for those who are willing to embrace the humility the lessons require. It talked about Peter, Jesus's disciple, and how his failures became tools of redemption in Jesus's hands."

"What does that mean?"

"I think first, that failing doesn't have to be the end. And that if I'm willing to take in the lessons of why I failed and be willing to admit fault in it, then I can learn, I can grow. I can stand up, bruised and muddy though I might be, and begin again. Do better the next round."

Kate let that take a couple of turns in her mind until it sank into her heart. It felt a little terrifying to inch toward a precipice of trying yet again—there was still so much hurt and disappointment in her heart. So many untangled things between them.

But she didn't want failure to be the end of their story.

"Think *we* can?" Her voice wobbled as she whispered the words.

Jacob studied her, the veil of his pride completely torn. In his eyes was a heartachingly beautiful blend of hope and humility. His fingers trailed her cheeks, then traced her hair. "I still don't know how, but"—his arms clutched around her again—"I hope so, Katie. I desperately hope that you're willing to try again, because I don't want this to be the end of us."

ThisBoondockingLife entry #23

There is so much wealth in things that have nothing to do with possessions.

We witness each new sunrise, the triumph of a new day as it reclaims the world from darkness.

There's a rhythm and beauty to work. A wise guy once told Jake "there is always dignity in work," and he was right. It's a gift, one that bestows purpose and dignity, strength and renewed ambition. And if we're doing it right, it inspires praise.

There are moments of being together. Just...being. No agendas. No rushing. No forced conversation in an effort to dull the exposure of silence. We have immersed ourselves in a life in which we are entirely exposed to each other...and wow! There is security in it. Can you imagine that? All of our beautiful, wonderful places and all of our ugly, broken places have been revealed, and here we are, still together. Better for it.

And then there are the sunsets, each one a new glory as the sun leaves us in a display of splendor, as if imprinting a promise of return. Such shows are ever faithful and yet never the same.

What more could I want? I am a rich woman! Very rich indeed.

Chapter Nineteen
(in which Jacob and Kate trace miracles)

The fire crackled in the steel ring the Salazars had lent, bouncing orange and yellow light against the calm night. Jacob inhaled, taking in the dry, cool air of the valley. It smelled of burning pine, with faint hints of citrus and earth. He smiled, easing back into the lawn chair. Next to him, Kate had been in her chair, studying the dome of stars above.

"What were you thinking?" he asked her, moving his hand toward hers. He didn't take it in his palm—he still felt shaky when it came to those normal married sort of touches, and he also felt Kate's hesitancy in them—but he brushed his fingers over the back of her hand. Their relationship had become a slow current toward something better, and he wasn't about to rush that. Wasn't going to force his wants and agenda, knowing from experience that was likely to come crashing down around them.

Kate looked from the sky above to him, her gaze stalling on his. "When? Now?"

"No, though I'm curious about that too." He anchored his hand on the arm of his chair. "What were you thinking when you bought Gert?"

Her attention moved toward the skoolie across from them, and a hint of a smile played on her lips. "I'm not sure."

"Not sure, or you don't want to tell me that she was your way out?"

"No. I don't want to say that."

"But it was true."

Staring now at the flames at their feet, Kate didn't answer.

"I can't blame you for that, Katie. I'm still amazed that you let me come with you, to be honest."

Now she turned to him, and he thought he caught a sheen in her eyes. "I've been thinking about something Sally said to me."

He wasn't sure what to make of her switch in topics, other than she didn't want to talk about it. "What was that?"

Leaning toward him, Kate anchored her chin on her hand, her elbow pressed into the chair arm. "She told me that what seems like the worst thing ever can turn into the biggest blessing of your life."

"Bryce said something like that—only that God has the ability to take away things that get in the way of us worshiping Him. And usually that's for our good."

Kate leaned back again, her chin tilted toward that sky. "I've been thinking a lot about that lately, since I got sick."

"Why since then?"

"Because for every hard blow we've taken, it seems like goodness met us in the heartache. That can't be coincidence, can it? I mean, think about it. You and I, we were pretty much done, and yeah, I bought Gert because I thought she was my out. But then the great Seattle disaster happened, and she was our soft-ish landing. That wasn't random. It just couldn't be."

Jacob chuckled. "True. And you bought it from the Millers. Two of the biggest, most gracious hearts God ever made. They took us in and showed the way. Not random."

"Right." A smile lifted her voice. "And then you started working for Salazar Farms. He pays you faithfully, treats you well, gives you seconds produce, and happened to have a nurse practitioner for a wife. Convenient, since I was kind of in the woods. Not random." Kate looked at him, and this time he was certain that there was glitter in her gaze. She reached across the space and slipped her hand over his. "And here we are. Figuring out this life together."

He turned his hand so his palm met hers and then lifted her fingers to his lips. "Not random." He kissed her knuckles. "Not a small thing." He kissed her fingertips. Then, he took the chance. Leaning, he closed the space of gentle night between them and brushed a soft kiss on her mouth. "A miracle," he whispered.

With her free hand, she touched his cheek and then moved to kiss him lightly. "A miracle," she repeated.

He held for another breath and then slowly backed away. Her hand stayed in his, their fingers woven together. Jacob inhaled another crisp breath. It smelled of firewood, of citrus, and of earth. He'd forever link that combined aroma with hope. Beautiful, miraculous hope.

Gratitude flooded his soul.

***

Kate would have never believed saying goodbye to one's employers would be so emotional. Then again, she'd never before lived this sort of life. The Salazars heaped them with two boxes of seconds, two bags of rice, and three ready-to-reheat-and-eat meals for their next adventure.

"Be safe," Anitra said to Kate, and then she turned to Jacob, shaking her finger at him. "And don't you let her get that dehydrated again. You get sick, you hightail it right back here."

Jacob chuckled. "Yes, ma'am."

Señor Salazar stepped forward then, hand outstretched. "You have a place on my crew whenever you want it, *Huero*."

Traces of color dusted her husband's cheeks as he looked toward his feet and nodded. "I'm forever grateful to you."

"No need." Salazar smacked his shoulder. "You work hard, stay humble, and treat people like friends and family. That's success in life, no matter who you are or what you do."

Both Jacob and Kate stared at him, mouths open.

Salazar laughed. "You don't think Bryce made that up on his own, do you? He's way too young to be that wise." Brushing the silver at the temple of his head, he chuckled again. "I don't have this for nothing!"

Kate laughed alongside her husband, and when he draped an arm around her, she leaned into his side.

Señor Salazar sobered and stepped nearer. "Let us pray before you go."

Anitra nodded, and both Salazars lifted a hand—one to Jacob's head and one to Kate's. In a deep, smooth timbre, he spoke in

Spanish. The unfamiliar words came as a beautiful mystery to Kate's ears, and though she didn't understand his prayer, her skin prickled and her heart lifted. God knew what Señor Salazar said, and Kate had absolutely no doubt that his blessing was good. And then Señor Salazar translated his prayer, his gaze settling on first Kate and then Jacob as he spoke.

"May the Lord bless you and keep you. May the Lord make His face shine on you and be gracious to you; the Lord turn His face toward you and give you peace."

"Amen," Anitra said.

Señor Salazar cupped the side of Jacob's head, a hold that seemed more father-son in nature than employer-employee. "Amen."

Jacob gripped Salazar's outstretched arm and leaned toward the man. Kate stood nearly breathless. She'd never seen her husband respond that way, hadn't ever witnessed him hug even his dad.

"You'll never know all you've done," Jacob said.

It took all of Kate's self-control to withhold her tears as she moved to hug Anitra.

The woman received her. "Go in peace, *mi niña bendita*, and live."

Blessed indeed. With God's gaze upon them and His good help—something Kate had foolishly doubted all this time—they would do exactly that.

***

Jacob studied the map, tracing the highlighted path he and Kate had agreed on. There was something truly thrilling about holding the glossy paper of an old-school map in his hands, fingering their progress as they went. They'd left behind the Joshua Tree National Park, passed from California into Arizona, driven through the desert plains, and had reached the scattered pines of the Coconino National Forest. They'd boondock there for a few nights before continuing north to the Grand Canyon.

Anticipation hummed in his body as he'd watched the changing landscape pass by. When they'd discussed going back to Sugar Pine for the family gathering Jacob's mother had planned,

Kate had shared with him her original plan to visit the national parks. He'd latched on to that idea like it had been the best thing he'd ever heard. Why hadn't he thought of it? Jacob's entire outline for this boondocking life had been to find ways to work to pay off his debts, and he still intended to do so. But there had to be joy in that life. He needed to find a way to *live*. And Kate, once again, proved to be his lifeline. They had the time, and Kate's books were doing well, better than she'd predicted. Why not take advantage of this boondocking life the way Bryce and Sally had?

Together they'd mapped out a plan for the next two weeks. The Grand Canyon. A couple of days near Lake Tahoe. Then a long-overdue visit with their families. They'd be lying if that last part didn't make them anxious. But.

They'd be in it together. Really together. Jacob had never felt strength like this in facing the challenging, hard things in life. Kate was *with* him on this. In all his struggles growing up, what he'd really longed for was to be seen. Kate saw him—the good, the bad, and the really, *really* bad—and there she was, still with him.

She'd told him she'd tried to make him her Prince Charming. The one who rescued her out of a miserable life. The truth was, she'd rescued him more than once. Not in a salvation sort of way, but in a show-him-a-different-way-to-be sort of way.

Two are better than one.

He'd read that in his morning devotions a couple days back, and it had struck him that it had taken him losing everything— failing epically—to really understand that. God hadn't made him to forge his own brilliant way alone, and He hadn't left him to do it that way either. Kate had been a gift, one of partnership. Not a prize, though she was certainly proving how much of a treasure she really was. She was his complement, his very capable partner in this life. The one he wanted to laugh with. The one he could entrust his whole heart to, even the broken parts.

And those broken parts were healing. That soft, beautiful thought took him back to the night before they'd left the valley...

What had started with a tentative kiss had become a night full of passion and surrender, of giving and receiving and finding oneness again. Later, when she lay wrapped in his arms, he'd asked her why now? What had he done wrong before, and what had changed? With tears and faltering words, Kate had confessed her fears, that she'd end up brokenhearted all over again, losing his affection. And also, she was terrified of becoming pregnant again, only to grieve the loss of yet another baby alone.

Her words had pierced, and they had cried together. He hadn't known how much she needed him to share his own grief over their losses with her. Hadn't meant to leave her feeling isolated.

As a pang echoed through his chest yet again, Jacob inhaled, looking at his wife's profile. As she navigated toward their next destination, her face shone with a quiet contentment.

Man, he loved her. *Help me love her better.*

She glanced at him in the rearview mirror.

"Did I tell you I heard from my mom this morning?" Kate's question broke miles of comfortable silence between them. She bit her bottom lip, and her brows knitted.

Not good signs.

"No, I don't think so."

She nodded.

"More threats?"

"Yes."

"Can I read it?"

"I was hoping you would. I haven't responded to her." She dug her phone out of her vest pocket and passed it back to him while maintaining visual on the road.

Jacob took the cell, punched in her passcode to unlock the screen, and opened the text from her mom.

Me n Rodney need help. Don't tell me there's no money this month. I ain't dumb. You and that rich husband of yours keep holding out and that's shameful. This time, I ain't gonna be so nice. Remember, I still hold your secret from those richy-rich in-laws of yours. I don't have to keep my mouth shut.

"Nice," Jacob growled. He looked up from the screen and found Kate gripping the steering wheel with way more force than necessary. Holding his gaze on her, he waited until she glanced up to the mirror again. "We've come a long way, Katie."

She rolled her lips together and visibly swallowed.

Leaning toward her, he laid a hand on her shoulder. "When we tell the truth, she can't hold the lies over us anymore."

Blinking, Kate nodded. "I know," she whispered.

"I'll tell my parents. You don't have to."

"No, I need to come clean. It's long overdue."

He knew every bit of courage that took for her to admit and how much more it would take for her to follow through. And he was proud of her for it. "I'll be there with you, then."

Up ahead was a rest stop. Kate guided Gertrude to the exit and into a long slant parking spot. Once the brake was secured and the engine shut off, she turned to face him. "I should have done this long ago, just like you wanted me to. There were so many things that I should have done differently, and maybe I wouldn't have lost everyone's respect." Her look moved toward her toes, and then she peeked back at him. "Including yours."

He slid off the bench and onto the top step at her feet, covering her knee with one hand. "You haven't lost anything."

"You told me to tell the truth though."

Pulling in a long breath, Jacob paused a moment to pray for wisdom. Not a well-practiced move for him, but he'd been working on it.

"Jake, why didn't you tell them back then?" Soft curiosity was in her eyes.

He moved his hand from her knee and pushed his fingers into the loose tresses of her hair. "Because I was selfish," he whispered.

"I don't understand."

"*I* wanted you, Kate. You clung to me because I kept your secret. Telling my family the truth, telling Jackson, was a risk I wasn't willing to take."

As understanding played in her expression, her blue eyes sheened. She curved a hand around his neck, brushed her thumb over his ear, and leaned to meet his mouth. These soft, warm kisses they'd shared in the past few days were tender, timid, and sweet. Not entirely satisfying—because when it came to Kate, Jacob would never have enough—but promising.

Kate pulled away slowly, tipping her forehead to his. "I would have chosen you, Jake."

He hoped so. Part of him felt like he'd never know for sure, but that was his own fault.

"I choose you now." Her mouth found his again, and in her deepened kiss, he found no room to doubt.

There was a lot about their story Jacob wished hadn't happened. Choices he would take back in a heartbeat if given the chance.

But this...this redeemed all the missteps and tears, the long, hard nights of anger and disillusionment.

There were still aches, still sorrows, and no doubt there would be more to come.

But.

This life he and Kate shared now, he would never regret.

ThisBoondockingLife entry #23

> *Some might jump into this way of living as a means of escape. We are all cowards in something, if we're being honest.*
>
> *At some point, most of what we'd rather not face will catch up with us. Maybe by the time it does, we will have gained the courage we need to face them. Courage inspired by the grandeur of creation, witnessed firsthand, absorbed rather than shoved to the periphery. Courage gleaned from the simplicity of life stripped down to the bare essentials.*
>
> *We all need this courage, because the thing is, one can only run for so long.*
>
> *Jake and me...*
>
> *Well, let's just say that there are some things we must face. No life is perfect, after all. Even this boondocking life, as amazing as it is.*
>
> *Deep breath. I'm inhaling all that courage.*

Chapter Twenty
(in which Jacob and Kate go home)

Kate shut her eyes as she finished her entry for *ThisBoondockingLife*. Pressing into the very recent memories of the spectacular Grand Canyon, she drew in that deep breath she'd just written about. She and Jake had spent four days camping nearby, splurging on campsite fees at the national park, enjoying hot showers, lingering mornings over coffee and cinnamon rolls—another splurge—and being repeatedly amazed by the views as they hiked the area. Not to mention languid nights spent wrapped up in each other's arms.

There were simply no words for it all.

Sitting on that side bench while Gert took them northwest toward Sugar Pine, back toward a life that had seemed so dark and broken, Kate steadied her resolve. She glanced at Jake in the driver's seat and felt the warm, rough grip of his hand holding hers. That was how they'd ended their hikes over the past few days, his firm grip clutching her hand.

Ah, courage. There it was. And that was astounding. She and Jake had started this journey as jagged pieces that didn't work. Didn't even seem to like each other, for the most part. And now...now simply the memory of him holding her hand, and the knowledge that he would do so again, gave her the gust of courage. A miracle, just like he'd said.

You do see! The thought lifted heavenward as a prayer. A praise. And a humble cry of repentance. She thought about what Bryce had said to Jacob about God stripping away things that got in the way of worship—and that was for the better. Indeed, Bryce was right.

God had met her in the darkest places, the most hopeless circumstances. He'd revealed that He'd been there all along, waiting for her—for both of them—to *cease striving and know that HE is God!* With the sleeve of her flannel shirt, Kate wiped the falling tears from her cheeks.

She looked back at her laptop and reread her entry. At some point she needed to be honest with her rapidly growing audience and tell them the real reason *ThisBoondockingLife* began. But not yet, and she had peace about that. One mountain at a time. Right now, that peak would be facing their families. A task that would begin by sundown.

***

"Well, lookie who showed up." Mom shifted to one hip on her mauve recliner. That was as much of a welcome as she was gonna muster. She smiled widely at Kate. "Did you bring a check this time?"

"Hi, Mom. It's nice to see you too." Kate balled her fists at her side, but at the warmth of Jake's hand on her lower back, she eased off the tense edge her mother had immediately set her on.

"Good evening, Vera." Jake's calm voice eased Kate further.

"Bless this mess, if the prince himself ain't graced my trailer with his magnanimous presence." This time Mom kicked the footrest into the chair and actually stood. "I'd curtsy if it mean you'd quit holding out on me 'n' Rodney."

Wow, Mom had been soaking in bitterness something fierce. Clearly it hadn't helped that Kate's eventual response to Mom's threats had been a noncommittal *We'll talk when I get to Sugar Creek. Face to face.*

After Kate had sent that text, with Jake's knowledge, he'd squeezed her arm and said, "Let's pray about this until the time comes."

And they had. Every morning since they'd left the Coachella Valley, Jake had spent time reading by himself, and then he'd pour two fresh mugs of coffee, bring Kate one, and they'd pray together.

"Is Rodney around?" Jacob asked.

"He ain't." Mom scowled.

"Can you reach him?"

"What for?"

"Kate and I have thought long and hard about this situation. You need to know that as of tomorrow morning, there will be no more lies to my family about who you are or where Kate is from."

Mom's face drained to a ghastly pallor, which was replaced by a violet-red hue with astonishing speed. Her scowl reached rage levels, and her pinned lips turned white around the edges. With lightning flashing in her eyes, she stepped nearer, her glare pinned on Kate. "Is there no end to your selfishness, girl?"

A tremble shook Kate's core. Jake stepped closer, sliding his hand from her back so that his arm was securely around her. *Courage. God, help me know what to do, and to do it.*

"Mom, this needs to end."

It seemed, by that awful, silent glare, that her mother actually hated her in that moment. Still, Kate plunged forward. "You need help, and Jacob and I want to help you."

The ugliness faded from Mom's expression. "Oh. Well then—"

"We're not going to keep giving you money, Mom."

"What?" The word came out loud and sharp, like a slap.

"You and Rodney need to learn how to manage what you have, and you need to stop gambling."

"I don't gamble."

"How many lottery tickets did you buy last month? How much did you spend at keno?"

"That ain't gambling. I ain't never fed the slots."

Kate shut her eyes and resisted the urge to growl. "It's an addiction, and it needs to stop."

"Listen here, young lady." Mom stepped closer still. "I ain't listen to no fancy-pants girl telling me how to live my life. I raised you, miss priss. Went with your lies, pretended in front of the prince's parents to be your wealthy mother. Even spoke all high and mighty. I kept your secrets, both of you. This is some gratitude, seeing how you wouldn't be where you are now if it weren't for me."

Jacob tucked Kate in closer. "We never should have asked that of you, Vera. It was very wrong. And as Kate said, we're willing to help you. We want to. But there will be terms."

"Terms?"

"Yes. Terms. Truth is, we don't have much money either, and Kate can't just give you her book royalties anymore. We live on them now. The other truth is, you and Rodney are living an unhealthy and codependent life. You can deny that if you'd like—that's not up to either Kate or me—but what is up to us is how we offer you help. And as I said, as of tomorrow morning, bright and early, everything Kate and I lied about will be revealed to my family. You won't be able to blackmail your daughter anymore."

"I never blackmailed my own daughter!"

Kate stared at her mom, incredulous. The woman lost it. She stomped like an out-of-control child and screamed at them.

"I ain't a bad person, and I never done such a horrible thing!"

Suddenly, Mom was sobbing. She doubled over and nearly crumbled to the floor. Jacob scuttled forward, catching Mom's pudgy elbow with one hand and keeping her upright with his other arm curled around her. Kate moved to her other side, and together they guided her back to the sagging, stained chair.

"My chest! Oh, it hurts!" Mom clutched at the worn-out and misshapen fabric of her shirt. "I'm dying! I'm dying. Look at me! You're killing me!"

From her side of the recliner, Kate looked up. Jacob met her gaze and gave a subtle, silent shake of his head. He was right. This was another ploy.

"Just breathe, Mom."

"I can't!"

"You're talking, so you can breathe. Calm down and breathe."

"I can't! I can't! I can't!"

Jacob stood straight, and Kate followed his lead.

"Mother, we're not doing this. If we can't have a conversation, then there's no point in us staying." Kate stepped around the chair and to Jacob's side. His hand gripped hers, and they walked toward the door.

"Wait!" Suddenly Mom wasn't breathless and in agony.

Kate turned, eyebrow sliding upward.

Mom slumped against her hideous chair. Defeated. "Come back."

Turning, Jacob looked first at Kate and then at her mother. "One more fit like that and this is done."

Anger carved gorges in Mom's face, but she nodded. "What are your terms?"

"You get Rodney here, and then we'll talk about them together," Jacob said. "But as a preview, here's a couple of ground rules: If you ever threaten my wife again, this is over. If you ever throw a fit like that again, we're done. Clear?"

Mom swallowed, turning to look at the ginormous screen of her television.

"Vera."

"I got it," Mom snapped.

Kate inhaled a long breath of stale air. It carried the pungent odor of bodies long overdue a soap bar, socks well past ripe, and the strong suggestion that the garbage needed removed.

This was going to be a long, hard night. She could only pray it didn't end with cut ties.

***

The predawn air hit Jacob with a crisp hint of icy water and fresh pine. He stepped out of Gert, facing east. Weak yellow light fingered through the pine tops, the promise of a new day. Thank goodness, because yesterday had been a long one.

He shut the door quietly and hoped Kate would sleep until the sun had risen fully, drenching the old picnic spot near Sugar Creek with warm spring light. His wife certainly could use the extra rest. Dealing with her mom and Rodney yesterday had been exhausting for him—he couldn't imagine how Kate felt. Likely like a rag wrung out a few too many times. But in the end, they'd made headway. He hoped. Rodney eventually agreed to tell them what his monthly disability amounted to, and from there they were able to forge a budget and a plan.

Walking toward the swiftly moving spring waters of the creek, Jacob shook his head as he remembered Rodney's protests about the budget.

"Make a plan and work it—ain't that what they say, mister big?" Rodney had challenged Jacob when asked how he intended to pay bills. "That's what I done. I'm working my plan."

"Keno and lottery tickets aren't a plan, Rodney. They're a delusion."

"False." Rodney shoved a meaty finger in Jacob's face. "Odds gotta run my way at some point. Just gotta stay the course, as they say."

"How long have you been holding out on that?"

Rodney didn't answer.

"This course you're set on has put you in continuous crisis. And trust me, sir. I get it. It's not fun." Jacob tapped opened letters spread out on the table in front of them. "You're staring at a notice that your electricity is going to get shut off, and a third

notice on your overdue lot lease. Know what happens after that?"
Jacob knew. Intimately, he knew exactly what happened when
you ignored third notices.

A hard silence settled between them, and Jacob glanced at Kate.
She sat next to her mom, staring at her knuckles on the table.
Man, he wished this wasn't something they had to do—and
more, he wished she hadn't had to deal with this disaster on her
own all this time. He should have been in this with her sooner.
Also, he suspected she felt the sting of their own financial failures
in that moment—they'd lived through repossession and
foreclosure. His business speculation hadn't been a whole lot
different than Rodney's habitual gambling.

Humility had flooded him there, and it somehow made sorting
through the mess more bearable. They'd forged through the
tension, laid out a budget, scheduled times when Jacob would call
to ensure bills got paid, and made an agreement that he and Kate
would line up a grocery delivery service so at least they'd know
that her mom would be eating decent food. However, their
negotiations came to a screeching halt when Kate suggested help
for the gambling addiction. At that impasse, they'd let it go.
Maybe they shouldn't have, as this was likely not going to resolve
with a simple budget and a few phone calls, but at the moment
they had what seemed a start. Granted, it was a tenuous
beginning. He had no illusions that the plan would work
unhindered. But it was a start.

At the edge of the water's boundary, Jacob knelt and cupped his
hands. While the sun fingered his exposed neck with teasing
warmth, he splashed his face several times with the mountain-
fresh stream, cold though it was. A deep shiver ran over him, and
adrenaline flooded his veins. Standing, he looked back toward the
eastern sky. Golden light danced over the evergreen treetops,
cheery and hopeful as anything.

Jacob breathed in that hope. Heaven knew he needed it.

Time to go face the next hard task. He ran his hands through
his hair and looked up. "Go with me there too?"

He knew God would.

One of his Bible readings had been Joshua 1:9. *Be strong and courageous. Do not be afraid; do not be discouraged, for the LORD your God will be with you wherever you go.* The words, then and now, summoned an image of Connor, the brother who forever faced hard things with faith-deep courage. Jacob looked forward to seeing him later that day, as Connor and Sadie were scheduled to arrive sometime after lunch. But he had things to take care of before then. Hard, necessary things that required faith-deep courage.

Striding toward Gert, he laid hold of the Grom and pushed it across the bridge before he kick-started the engine. The drive toward the Murphy home wasn't long—up the hill, through several deep curves on the mountain road, and then the left turn into that familiar drive. Once parked in front of Dad's workshop, he cut the engine and pulled his phone from his jacket pocket while doing a quick scan of the vehicles parked closer to the house. Yes, Jackson was there too. Deep breath.

He found Jackson in his contact list and opened a new text. *Morning. Are you up?*

Two days before, Jacob had made contact with Jackson, double-checking that he and Kenzie were still planning to go to Mom and Dad's. Jackson had said yes and then asked the same of Jacob and Kate—and had seemed genuinely positive when Jacob confirmed that they would be there too. At the end of that exchange, Jacob asked if they could meet privately. Jackson thought that was a good idea.

Standing there in the chilly spring morning, Jacob had second thoughts about whether it was a good idea. He and Jackson never saw eye to eye. He couldn't even say why for sure, except that their personalities were so different, but he knew the two of them had never mixed well.

Man, this was gonna be hard. It could end badly.

I'm up. Got a couple of travel mugs full of coffee. Meet you on the ridge?

No going back now. *Right behind you.*

Jacob sent his text and then flipped to his newly acquired Bible app. There was something about the printed Word that he had quickly come to prefer—likely because the temptation of distraction was significantly decreased with a physical book—but it was good to have the app for moments such as this. He tapped through a few screens until he came to Psalm 46, the very psalm he'd read before shutting off the light last night. Slowly, he read the words out loud. Phrases resounded in his heart: *Come see what the LORD has done... He makes wars cease... He says, "Be still and know that I am God."*

With a quick slide of his thumb, he switched to his texting screen. After pulling up Bryce's name, he punched out a simple request for prayer—one he was certain Bryce would fulfill without even questioning why—and then looked back at the house. Squeezing his phone in his palm, Jacob tipped his face upward and shut His eyes. "Give me the courage to be humble and honest, and please, *please* cease this war."

With that prayer, Jacob strode around the Murphy house, through the backyard, and set his feet on the trail toward the ridge. This journey had been a long time coming, and he found he had been given just enough courage to make that last climb.

Jackson sat on the wide boulder at the top, his attention focused on the warming sun rising in the eastern sky. At the sound of Jacob's approach, Jackson twisted to face him. For a tense, silent moment, his younger brother studied Jacob as if he was piecing a puzzle. Determining how this meeting should begin.

"Morning." Jacob stopped three feet short of the boulder.

One side of Jackson's mouth hitched up, as if he'd decided to approach this uncommon moment with a good nature. He lifted a hand, which held a silver travel mug, and held it toward Jacob. "Good morning, Jacob."

It took a step forward to reach the offered coffee. "Thanks."

"Just Mom's regular brew—nothing fancy."

Jacob shrugged. "Fancy coffee is overrated. And way too expensive."

One dark brow pushed into Jackson's forehead. "Yeah? Since when?"

"Probably since always. But for me, since about March, I suppose."

"What happened in March?"

Jacob's carefully constructed world had collapsed, that was what. He wasn't sure he wanted this conversation to start there though. Not that he didn't intend to tell Jackson, and the rest of the family, what was going on. But not just yet. He didn't want to start this confession on a page of pity—that didn't seem right.

He looked over the dew-tinged treetops that draped the slope below them. Sunlight grabbed the droplets, transforming them from common water to shimmering diamonds. A draw of breath filled him with crisp morning air scented by pine and dew and earth.

Behold, I am making all things new... That had been a reading from over a week before.

"What's going on, Jacob?" Jackson stood, stuffing his now-free hand into his puffer vest pocket.

Jacob faced Jackson squarely. "I think it's time for you and me to be honest."

"Okay..."

"Actually, it's time for *me* to be honest with you. About what happened with Kate."

Jackson pulled his hand from his pocket and held it up. "Look, I don't really care—"

"I know. You've moved on, and I'm glad for you. But I need to tell you the truth. And...and to apologize for how everything happened."

Brows drawn quizzically inward, Jackson stared at him. "You and Kate okay?"

"We're...we're getting there. But we haven't been. Not for a long time."

"I'm sorry, Jacob." Sincere pity softened Jackson's look. "I hope that I wasn't—"

"You weren't. I mean, the things between me and Kate weren't your fault. You didn't do anything wrong by us."

He looked to the ground, and then Jackson rubbed his neck.

"I'm not sure that's true. I was pretty angry."

"You had a right to be."

Slowly, Jackson's eyes met Jacob's again. "Why didn't you just tell me, instead of sneaking around behind my back for weeks?"

"I wanted to." Jacob stopped, not wanting to pass the blame onto his wife. "No, that's not true." He sighed and swallowed. "Hear me out, okay?"

"I'm listening."

"Kate is from Sugar Creek."

"I know that. Her aunt has a cabin—"

"No, Jackson. There's no remote cabin. No reclusive aunt. And her mother isn't a successful, wealthy businesswoman. Kate grew up in Sugar Creek Cove."

Again, Jackson's brows folded. "Sugar Creek Cove?"

"The trailer park across the bridge. Her mom still lives there in a 1971 double-wide that smells like body odor, forty-year-old carpet, and week-old garbage. She lives on cheap box foods and a delusional hope that the lottery is going to kick in for her one day."

Jackson's mouth gaped. "Kate? Why did she lie?"

"It's a long story that basically comes down to her wanting to reinvent herself. She was ashamed of her life and angry with her mom, and she didn't want to be known as the trailer-park girl anymore, so she transferred schools and created a whole new story for herself. But it wasn't true."

"Why didn't she tell me?"

"You were part of her new life, and she was desperate for it to work."

"Why did she tell you?"

Jacob drew a long breath. "I took her home one night, after your last basketball game. I saw her walk to the bus stop alone and didn't feel good about that. When she told me to just drop her off at the bridge, I refused. It was dark, and she was alone... Anyway, I pretty much told her she wasn't leaving the car until we were at her front door, wherever that was."

Taking it in, Jackson nodded.

"Sitting in front of the trailer she called home that night, she told me why she'd lied, and to be honest, her story kind of broke my heart. Then she begged me not to tell you. I told her that wasn't right, and she said she'd tell you, but then..." Jacob drew in another long breath. "Then things sort of got complicated, I guess."

"You took her home at night, after we'd hang out, didn't you? When she said her aunt was out there waiting for her, it was you."

Jacob nodded.

"Why?"

"I wanted to protect her."

"Jacob, you know it wouldn't have mattered to me if she told me where she lived."

He nodded, looking at the ground. Pine needles littered the damp earth at his feet. The slim hope that had welled within him earlier began to dry. Soon it'd fall, just like those brown pine needles lying dead against the ground.

"Why didn't *you* just tell me the truth?"

"Because I knew it wouldn't matter to you." Jacob couldn't look at his younger brother.

"What does that mean?"

After a long moment, Jacob forced himself to meet Jackson's eyes, a mix of regret and resentment surging through his veins. "You were popular and funny and charming and had everything going for you. All I had was her secret."

Jackson's scowl deepened, and he turned toward the sunrise again, giving Jacob his back. For several hard breaths, Jacob stood rooted, uncertain what to do. Finally he decided there was only one thing he could do, and then it was up to Jackson.

"I'm sorry, Jackson. It was a selfish, rotten thing for me to do."

"I'm your brother, Jacob." Jackson turned to pin him with a heated look. "How could you do that to your brother?"

Jacob felt himself shrink. "I just wanted *her*. That's not a good reason, but it's all I have."

With his left hand, Jackson rubbed his tight jaw, and then paused midmotion, his thumb going to the wedding band on his fourth finger. The anger in his expression faded, and he sighed. "It doesn't matter much now, does it?"

"Yeah. It does." Jacob motioned between them. "For you and me, it still matters. For you and Kate, it matters. Look, we've never been close, and I know that I carry a good share of that on my own shoulders. But you and Kate, you were good friends, and she regrets deeply how much she hurt you."

"It wasn't her." Jackson shook his head. "Jacob, I was over her before you were even married. She was a girl I dated in high school. That's all. There was never any promises between us, never an *I love you*. Nothing but that she was pretty and would laugh at my goofiness. But you—*you're* my brother."

Jacob felt like a deer pinned to the ground. Shot with a kill blow and bleeding out. There was no remedying this. The moment was hopeless shame and irrevocable mistake. He rubbed his unshaven face and nodded. "I know. I know, and I'm sorry."

The silent tension between them throbbed. But then Jackson moved. He closed the gap between him and Jacob and gripped Jacob's elbow. "We're brothers."

With a jolt, Jacob looked from the tips of his shoes to Jackson's face. The lines of anger and hurt had smoothed, and Jackson released Jacob's arm. He held an offer of a handshake between them. A crushing sense of unworthy relief rushed through him as Jacob took that offer. Jackson jerked him forward and wrapped his other arm around Jacob's shoulder.

"We're brothers," he repeated.

Jacob couldn't respond for the boulder of emotion in his throat, but he squeezed the hand that still gripped his. Jackson released him, and they stepped apart.

They stood side by side, both turned back toward the sunrise. A gentle breeze danced upward from the valley, setting the treetops in motion and brushing against Jacob's skin.

Cleansing and full of fresh hope.

"Speaking of brothers." Jackson nudged Jacob's arm with his elbow. "One of ours just got married. Know what that means?"

"Uh, we have a new sister-in-law?"

"No. I mean, yes, but that's not what we're talking about here. Come on, Jacob. Who am I?"

Jacob chuckled, enjoying the unfurling of tense muscles and the whisking away of almost a decade's worth of bad feelings between Jackson and himself. "You're the prankster."

"Exactly. Let's not forget it." Jackson sat down on the boulder again. "Wanna help on this one?"

"Think that's possible for this stiff fun-hater?"

"Learn from the master."

Jacob chuckled. "What do you have in mind?"

"The trick is to know your mark, brother." Jackson tapped his temple. "What do we know about Connor?"

"He feels overly responsible for everyone."

"Exactly. So we need a mountain lion, a bloody brother, and a clear trail."

"When you say mountain lion, you don't actually mean—"

Jackson swatted the air, waving off Jacob's tenuous question. "Course not. Just a recording. YouTube is gold."

"Right. And which brother will be the bloody brother?"

With a wide grin, Jackson settled his look dead on Jacob. He raised his mug. "To the one he'll never suspect."

Jacob laughed and clunked his own mug against Jackson's. "Let's do it."

ThisBoondockingLife entry #25

> There's a lot wrong in the world. So, so much,
> and I'm not saying we should just ignore all of
> that. But I keep coming back to this these
> days:
>
> There are some amazing people God put on
> this earth. Truly, utterly amazing.
>
> Makes me aspire to be one of them.

Chapter Twenty-One
(in which new beginnings are possible)

Jacob brought a paper cup of spiced chai when he returned to
the skoolie, and his heart turned over with a warm, gooey
sensation when she sat up, her golden hair a beautiful morning
mess and sleepiness still in her lovely expression.

"What is that glorious smell?" She yawned and pushed her hair
back from her face.

Bending to kiss her forehead, Jacob inhaled the warm smell of
his bride. She was crisp sunshine and oranges left out in the warm
spring sun. "Mmm... I like this glorious smell more," he
whispered.

Kate tipped her face so he could brush her lips with his. It was
like a honeymoon do-over, and he savored every moment of it.

Thank You, God. Thank You for all of it...

Scrambling against the mattress, Kate adjusted the pillow at her
back and leaned against it. Her blue eyes smiled at him as Jacob
lowered to sit near her legs. He offered her his gift. "I thought
maybe you missed these."

She'd purchased one at least twice a week. He had paid enough attention to at least remember that.

Rapture lighted her expression as she took the cup and breathed in the warm, spicey scent. Spiced chai wasn't Jacob's thing—he'd pass on that drink every time. But seeing her smile like that...

With a quick lean forward, she kissed his cheek. "You spoil me, Jacob Murphy."

"Ha. We both know that's not true." He caught her by the back of her head and snatched another kiss. "But I'm grateful for the chance to do better."

Their noses brushed, and she pressed her forehead against his. "Me too."

The sound of a car crossing the bridge that spanned the creek had Jacob pulling away sooner than he wanted. He stood, leaving Kate to sip on her warm indulgence while he moved the shade on a side window to see if he recognized the vehicle.

And he did. "It's Connor."

"Connor, your brother?"

"Yeah, and I'm guessing that's Sadie with him." A spiral of excitement worked through him, something that he hadn't experienced when seeing his family in way too long. Jacob grinned and looked at Kate.

She was blushing but returned his smile. "Keep them occupied for a few minutes?"

"Of course." He zipped his jacket up a little more and sent her a wink before descending the steps and exiting their unusual little home.

"Jacob!" Connor's enthusiastic call came before his brother had even fully stepped from his car.

Later Jacob would rerun that moment, counting it as another new beginning. Another gift of grace. "Connor." He crossed the space from the skoolie to Connor's vehicle and embraced the brother Jacob knew beyond all doubt had been the prayer warrior he and Kate had desperately needed.

"How are you?" Connor asked.

It was refreshing to be able to look a brother in the eye and feel no shame or resentment. "We're good. Kate's just getting dressed—she'll be out in a minute."

Connor smiled. "Perfect. In the meantime—" He rounded the nose of the car and met his own wife near the passenger door. "Do you remember Sadie?"

"I do." It'd been a long while since he'd seen the girl Connor had briefly dated in high school. She looked different, maybe a little worn. But lovely still. "I remember her as Sadie Allen."

"Murphy." Connor's tone was firm and pleased. "Sadie Murphy now. And this"—he bent to lift the little boy standing near Sadie's leg—"is our son, Reid. Reid, this is your uncle Jacob."

A beat of silence settled between them. Then Sadie nudged the boy in Connor's arms. "What do you say, buddy?"

Reid tucked as close as he could to Connor's shoulder. "Hi," he said quietly.

"Hi, Reid. It's nice to meet you." Jacob felt an instant connection with the shy little man. Even so, he wondered how Kate would react to meeting their new nephew. Would it summon the hurt of their own ungranted wishes? He hoped not, but he wouldn't wonder silently this time. He'd find a time later, when they were alone, and seek her heart about it.

The click of the skoolie door stole their attention, and Jacob turned to see Kate take the last step down. She looked unsure—which for Kate often came off as perhaps a little snooty. Jacob glanced at Connor, silently willing his brother to see Kate for who she actually was—a rather timid woman who wore a mask for courage.

"Kate!" Connor moved past Jacob until he was at Kate's side and then dropped an arm around her shoulders. "I'm glad to see you, sis."

Along with surprise, relief scrawled over Kate's expression, plain as anything Jacob had ever seen. While gratitude worked in his heart, Jacob glanced at Sadie. "How are you?"

"I'm...doing better, actually. This round has been surprisingly easier."

"I'm glad. Is Connor being good to you?"

A telling blush crept over Sadie's cheeks. "He's so good to me—

to both me and Reid."

Jacob had no doubt about it. And by the way Connor had looked at Sadie when he'd reintroduced her, Jacob had zero wonderings about whether or not his brother was happy in his marriage that had started as a matter of honor and duty. Connor loved his bride.

The group gathered loosely beside Gertrude's green panels, Kate sipping on her chai as she stole glances at Reid. The boy gave her a small smile, and by the expression in Kate's softening eyes, she was smitten. Jacob prayed there was a measure of healing in that.

They toured the skoolie, and Reid came out of his shell as they did. He scrambled on the bed, did a front summersault, and grinned straight at Kate. "Could I go on adventure someday too?"

Kate leaned in, her nose nearly brushing the little boy's, and smiled. "Isn't that a fun idea?"

Jacob glanced at Connor, who looked at Sadie. Sadie grinned and gave a subtle nod to Connor. Oh the possibilities! Hiking, fishing, finding dinosaur bones...so many things out there in this big wide world to captivate a little boy. But the topic was left to rest for the moment.

"Quite a gig you've come up with." Connor draped an arm around Kate's shoulder as she stood back up, and squeezed. As if this relationship was easy and natural. "I've been reading the blog—it's pretty addictive, actually. The pictures from the Grand Canyon were spectacular. And you made this old bus—"

"Skoolie," Kate corrected.

Connor chuckled. "Right. Skoolie. Sadie's been showing me your blog—we read every new entry you put up. You made the whole thing look like the charmed life."

A lovely blush tinging her cheeks, Kate shrugged. "Maybe it is."

Jacob looked at Connor with gratitude and then at Kate with pride. "She's gaining a pretty big following."

"I saw that," Sadie said, her reserved smile becoming more and more easy as time wore on. "Even have a few sponsors, right?"

"Yes," Kate said.

There was no measure to the relief Jacob felt. He was glad he'd listened to the intruding voice in his heart and had told at least one family member what they'd been doing the past couple of months, and that Connor proved to be a solid support.

Once again, Jacob thought on what Sally and Bryce had told them, that the worst things could turn into the best gifts.

After Sadie and Reid settled back into their seats of their car, Connor pulled a box of Jacob and Kate's rerouted mail from the trunk and passed it to Jacob, and then asked with deep sincerity if they were truly doing okay.

Jacob's gaze locked on Kate. "Yeah. We're really doing okay." His attention shifted to the rest of the day ahead. So far things had gone well. Just one more peak to summit—and it would be the hardest. "We're planning to sit down with Mom and Dad sometime today though. That's..."

Connor squeezed Jacob's shoulder. "It's time. You'll get through it. I'll be praying for you." He then strode back to Kate and wrapped her in a hug. "It's gonna be okay, sis. Promise."

***

Kate gripped Jacob's hand. Walking into the Murphy home had never felt quite this terrifying. Uncomfortable, yes. It had almost always been uncomfortable, and she was certain that her discomfort had made everyone around her uneasy as well. But this... This was a whole new level of awkward.

"Mom and Dad are in the family room," Connor said quietly. A couple of hours before, the same man had promised her everything was going to be okay. She'd latched on to his kindness and confidence and had believed him to be right. Right up until about twenty-five seconds ago. "Everyone else is off doing their own thing right now."

Likely by Connor's design. She should be grateful to him, but she only knew anxiety in that moment.

"I can stay, if you want," Connor said.

Jacob looked at Kate. She had no inclination either way, as she'd rather not have to do this at all. Her husband shook his head. "That's all right, but thanks. Is Jackson around?"

Kate's pulse galloped painfully at her husband's question.

"I can go find him, if you want?" Connor answered. "Did you—"

Jacob squeezed Kate's hand. "He and I talked this morning." He looked at her, his eyes searching. Gauging her reaction? "It's...in the past."

He'd talked to Jackson already? While Kate didn't understand why Jacob hadn't told her he was going to, the relief in his expression eased her rattled heart and defused any irritation she might have otherwise felt. "Really?"

"Really." That was all he offered.

She wanted to ask more. Did Jackson despise her for lying? Did he think she was just a gold digger, not worth caring one way or the other about?

"Katie." Jacob's low voice brought her out of her head.

She blinked, finding that Connor had left them alone.

"He doesn't hate either of us." A half smile tipped up one side of his mouth. "That's not Jackson's style anyway. He doesn't have the anger habit. Let's just get this out and be done with it. Once it's behind us, we all can truly move on."

Maybe they truly could. Connor knew the truth and didn't hate her. Had hugged her and called her *sis*. Now Jackson knew too and didn't despise her.

Kate filled her lungs, the breath an aromatic blend of strong coffee, sweet cinnamon rolls, and spiced oranges. "Okay," she whispered.

Her legs felt like rubber as she followed her husband into the open space of the Murphy family room. It was large, the ceiling vaulted with exposed beams. Two couches—each dressed in a white shabby-chic slipcover and loaded with soft buffalo-check throw pillows—bookended the stone fireplace. Scattered strategically throughout the rest of the room were a couple of wing-backed chairs, a heavy wooden rocker, and in the far corner, the overstuffed leather chair that was Kevin Murphy's favorite.

And there the man sat. He looked up from the book he had

balanced on one leg. "Jacob. Kate."

He stood, a reserved grin on his face. Stepping forward, he held a hand toward his son. Jacob took it and shook. Helen appeared then, stepping through the wide French door that connected the family room to her expansive sunroom. Biting her lip, she also smiled and stepped to Jacob for a hug.

And then she turned to wrap tentative arms around Kate. "How are you?"

Kate forced a swallow past the lump in her throat. She and Helen had made small strides forward the last time Kate had been here. Now...now what was about to ensue could cut back every small hope Kate had for ever finding friendship with this woman. "Fine," Kate whispered unconvincingly.

Helen studied Kate and then Jacob, her grin fading.

"Everything okay?" Kevin asked, clearly guessing that no, everything was not okay.

Jacob glanced at Kate and then cleared his throat. "We need to talk to you both."

"Oh dear, that sounds...ominous." Helen looked up at her husband and then stepped toward one of the couches. She motioned for Jacob and Kate to sit across from them. "Should I get coffee first?"

"No, we're good. Thank you though."

"Are you in trouble, son?"

"Not, not at the moment, I don't think. But we need to clear the air about some things."

Kate's fingernails bit into her palm as she clenched her hands. *Just get it out there so we can move on...* "I need to tell you the truth."

***

Startled, Jacob looked at her. He wanted to do this, though Kate had said she must face them with the truth. They were his parents, and he'd been complicit in the deception. Moreover, Kate was his wife, and over the past weeks he'd come to terms with the fact that he hadn't played his role as husband—protector and leader and support—very well at all. He'd been Adam in the garden, watching while Eve slipped into deception. Participating in the rebellion, then blaming her for all.

He wanted no more of that.

"I lied to you," Kate plunged forward, and Jacob drew in a sharp breath.

Mom sat back, mouth down. Dad's eyebrows lifted. Jacob braced a hand on her back, proud of her strength despite wanting to take this on himself. If she was this determined, then he wanted her to know he was right there with her, and he would own his own fault in all of it.

"I made up this charmed life," Kate continued. "I told you that I came from money, that my mother was a highly successful businesswoman, that she'd agreed to let me live with an aunt to finish high school. None of it was true. I grew up in the Sugar Creek Cove trailer park. My mom still lives there, and she is far from wealthy. She is a compulsive gambler and has been for a long time. I was never the girl Jackson thought I was."

Jaw slack, Mom blinked, her focus on Kate. "Why would you lie about that? Surely you realize no one here cares—"

"*I* cared."

The subtle crack in his wife's voice chipped at Jacob's heart. If Mom knew all of Kate's history—her mother's betrayal, then her best friend's, and how she was treated at her old school—Mom might understand. Certainly she would. His mother owned a tender heart. But Kate wouldn't offer excuses in this, he was sure.

He felt a small quake tremble through his wife as she continued. "I transferred to Sugar Pine High to reinvent my life. When Jackson asked me out that winter, I thought it was the beginning of a new kind of life for me"—Kate gestured to the great, beautiful room—"this kind of life. For a girl who grew up the way I did, this was a fantasy, and I was Cinderella. I didn't want to risk losing something I'd only ever dreamed of by telling Jackson that I wasn't who I'd told everyone I was. Then I met Jacob, and we kind of..."

"*I* pursued her," Jacob interrupted. He couldn't let her take on responsibility for the rest of it. That had been his failing. His. He should have had the strength and depth of character to do what was right for all of them back then. He hadn't. Instead, he'd dwelled in the fear that if Jackson knew the truth, *he'd* become her rescuing prince charming, and then Kate would be lost to Jacob. "At first I convinced myself that I was only keeping her safe, because I discovered her secret that first night we met. I made sure she got home at night. Gave her rides to school in the mornings. But it became clear quickly that wasn't all there was between us." Not by a long shot. From the very first night, there had been attraction. Jealousy and selfishness had acted as Jacob's guides from that point forward.

"Jacob." Mom's low whisper was all disappointment.

He deserved it, but feeling the exposure of his failures still pricked defensiveness to life. Setting his mind on humility, Jacob tamped that old fallback down. There was no real excuse for how he'd handled any of what had happened.

Dad cleared his throat. "I think we know the rest. It's been a shadow over this house long enough."

In the heavy look Dad settled on him, Jacob felt the full weight of responsibility he'd carried in upending relationships within the family. A strained silence gripped the room, and a glance told Jacob that Kate's bottom lip trembled. Again, the urge to excuse what he'd done rose up. Again, he battled it back.

Mom sighed and turned her eyes to Kate. "I don't understand why you continued to lie to us. Why didn't you just tell us the whole truth back when you—" Mom cut herself off and then planted her look back on Jacob, her frustration in him written on her knitted brow. "You paraded Kate's mother around at the wedding as if she was the woman Kate invented. You kept up the charade for years. Why?"

Jacob leaned forward, bracing his arms on his legs. He didn't have a good answer for that question, other than Kate didn't want his family to know the truth. She hadn't wanted anyone to know. Jacob wasn't going to say that though, because it would deflect responsibility to his wife. Instead, he moved forward, toward where they were now and why. He was determined Dad and Mom know that they lived in a skoolie, that he didn't have a consistent job, and hopefully he'd get to the light at the end of the tunnel: that losing everything had become the best worst thing that had ever happened to them.

"It gets worse than that. My big, successful business in Seattle was a sham. Nothing more than a gambler's delusional dream." He glanced at Kate, his heart now full of empathy for her mother. "I took on way too much debt, trying to look the success I wanted everyone to think I was." As heat washed over his head and neck, Jacob stared at his shoes. "In the end, I lost everything." Slowly, he lifted his head and looked at his dad. "Everything but Kate."

Turning, he found his wife's blue eyes, laden with held-back tears, looking up at him. Her hand slipped into his, and he felt the warmth of the miracle that had happened between them.

He should have lost her, but he hadn't. Instead they'd found a new place to begin again. Somewhere honest and simple and full of hope. A place far better than where they'd started.

After a beat of silence, Jacob looked back at his parents. Mom still battled her great disappointment—something she'd been battling when it came to Jacob for years, which had fueled Jacob's own resentment. For so long he'd thought his mother was so deeply disappointed in him because she favored Jackson. That hadn't been true though. Mom was disappointed in Jacob because Jacob was her son, and he'd willfully treaded a rebellious path. It had very little to do with Jackson or any of his brothers.

Dad's silence was the contemplative kind, the kind that was him sorting through the facts and looking for what was lying underneath it all. His brow furrowed deeply as he studied Jacob. "Is this you asking for money, son?"

Though asked calmly, the question plunged a walloping sting into Jacob's heart. He'd spent the past seven years parading pretention and creating canyons in his relationships. Suspicion would only be a natural response from anyone. But it still hurt to have his dad ask such a thing.

"No." Jacob's voice broke. He swallowed, rolling his fist tight as he fought to regain his emotions. "This is me and Kate asking for your forgiveness."

Immediately the stiff postures of the pair across from them sagged.

Jacob sniffed and then sat straight. "Kate was young, and her life had been hard disappointment up until she met Jackson—you might understand more if you saw what I had. But I knew better than to lie. I just didn't do better. Our choices made things hard, and we're still trying to find our way out of the darkness. But that's on us. I'm not asking for your understanding, and I can't give a good reason for why I did what I did—why we did what we did—because there isn't one." Kate's fingers trembled within his hand, and he squeezed it. "But neither of us want to live under the lies we told anymore. And both of us would very much like your forgiveness."

His heart hammered as he finished, and at his side, Kate sniffed.

"I really am so very sorry," she whispered.

At that, Mom's face crumbled. Tears brimmed over her blue eyes, and she stood, stepped around the coffee table that separated the two couches, and lowered onto the cushion beside Kate. Without a word, Mom folded her arms around Jacob's wife. Suddenly, Kate broke. She curled into Mom's embrace while quiet cries shook her frame, and Mom held her close.

Though she said nothing, every broken thing that had been stored in Kate's heart, in that moment, came gushing out. Jacob continued to hold her hand, and he could not stop the tears that rolled onto his cheeks. Dad was there then, sitting on the table in front of Jacob, gripping first his shoulder and then his head.

Jacob pressed into the strong arm that had tugged him near, knowing another miracle had happened.

He'd been forgiven. Again.

***

Kate wasn't exactly sure how to fit with the group of women who shared her last name. But today she was going to try. How could she not? Helen had held her with the tender love of a mother, let her cry without intruding with words, and then when the storm had subsided, wiped both Kate's tears and her own with a gentle smile. From that moment they had a new beginning. Kate was not about to squander that.

Five Mrs. Murphys piled out of Helen's minivan after she parked near Sugar Creek at the picnic spot. They'd left the brothers to embark on their planned hike—and something was definitely up with that, Kate was sure. Jackson Murphy didn't miss an opportunity for mischief. Times past, Jacob would have opted out of the group activity. Today, however, was a new day.

A smile played at Kate's mouth with that thought.

Helen scurried to walk beside Kate, slipping a hand through her arm as they strode toward Gert. "Tell me again what this lovely thing is called." An adventurous smile rang in Helen's voice.

"It's a skoolie—and her name is Gertrude."

"It's fantastic!" Lauren grinned widely, her hand unconsciously resting on her baby belly. "Matt will be so jealous."

"Matt?" Kenzie adjusted little Bobbie Joy in her Babybjorn. "Do not even show this to Jackson." She looked past Lauren and smiled at Kate. "You are the bravest among us."

Kate laughed, loving the way her anxiety died in the warmth of these women. "Bravery had nothing to do with it. Gert was a last resort, and if you want to know the truth, the first few weeks of living as boondockers was frankly horrible. There was burnt food, mud, and cold showers. Thank God He had us camping in the backyard of some very benevolent people at the very beginning, because if we had been left on our own on the outset, we likely would have killed each other."

Laughing, they'd arrived beside Gert's big green shell, and Kate unlocked the door. One by one, the women filed up and into her galley.

"It's adorable!" Lauren gushed. "Please tell me you've been blogging this."

"She has." Sadie spoke up in her quiet, shy way. She had left Reid with Grandpa Kevin to work on something that had to do with wood and nails, and it seemed to Kate that Sadie was also fumbling with how to fit in as the latest Murphy addition. As Kate met Sadie's soft gaze, she felt a kinship blossom between them.

"*ThisBoondockingLife* is becoming quite popular," Sadie said.

Four sets of eyes turned to Kate.

"Wow." Lauren's eyes glittered with admiration. "Two successful bloggers in the family now."

"How do you make it all work?" Helen asked. "I mean, you have to pay for gas and groceries, right?"

"Right." Kate leaned against the sun-warmed dashboard as Lauren and Helen sat down on the bench. Mackenzie stood near the bed at the back, and Sadie leaned against the counter. "Jacob is a genius with a spreadsheet, and the people we first stayed with—Bryce and Sally—had boondocked for two years. They gifted us with everything they knew and helped us come up with a budget and a plan. It was scary though, because my book royalties can be unpredictable."

"Wow, though!" Lauren, as always, was bright sunshine and enthusiasm. "How great that you can write and earn an income while you're traveling. That's awesome, Kate!"

Kate felt her smile grow. "Thanks. It wasn't really something we ever thought about, but when things fell apart in Seattle, it was all we could think to do. Honestly, it's super hard. But we're getting it, and it's been a really humbling and amazing experience so far."

"What does Jacob do?" Helen wanted to know.

"He worked as a seasonal picker for about six weeks. The past two weeks, we were playing tourists though. He's been managing marketing for me also, and he's *way* better at it than I am, so that's been good."

Surprise and then pride filtered through Helen's expression. "Such a unique opportunity for you guys. Do you like it now?"

"Now? Yes." Kate's answer surprised her. She hadn't yet stopped to reevaluate this new life she and Jacob were living. But truthfully, yes, she liked where they were now and what they were doing. She liked who they were becoming. "It's been...I don't know the word. It's been like a reset for us. Maybe a detox from the noxious world we'd created. We've redefined what success is. What luxury and being blessed means. It used to mean going out and buying a ridiculously expensive purse or something equally as frivolous. Now, luxury is a hot shower. A simple, satisfying meal shared beside a crackling campfire. It's making new friends and discovering there are some tremendously generous people in the world. People who inspire us to be better humans ourselves. And it's holding hands under a starlit sky, feeling gratitude rather than angst."

A contemplative silence followed Kate's response. Helen reached for Kate's hand and squeezed. "And wealth? What is that to you now?"

Kate thought of Bryce and Sally, of Anitra and Horatio Salazar, and a glow of admiration burned in her heart. Their true wealth had nothing to do with property or things, with bank accounts or positions. "Wealth has become a beautiful combination of contentment, of generous living, and a love for honest work, all upheld by a wisdom that comes from God—a knowledge that is firmly grounded in understanding Who really owns it all. Just the other morning, Jacob read out of first Chronicles 29."

Kate reached across the dash, retrieving Jacob's Bible. "It says, 'Yours, LORD, is the greatness and the power and the glory and the majesty and the splendor, for everything in heaven and earth is yours.' The verses go on to say that honor and wealth and power all come from God." She looked up again. "True wealth is rare, but now that I've seen it, all the money in the world can't compare."

Nothing short of motherly pride shone from Helen's teary smile.

"You didn't blog that," Sadie said. "I think you should."

Self-conscious, Kate laughed quietly. "Perhaps tonight. Who am I, though, to write such lofty things?"

Sadie shrugged and winked. "You're the writer of ThisBoondockingLife—the one who God has entrusted with such an adventure."

The five Mrs. Murphys gathered in Gertrude the skoolie laughed.

Kenzie cradled little Bobbie Joy's head and kissed her fine ginger hair. "What's next for you two?"

Even as an ache pulled in Kate's heart at the sight of mother and child, a movement of worship swayed through her mind— *praise God, He has provided again!* In that space of pain and praise, Kate felt another stitch of healing weave in her heart. God had proven Himself trustworthy in this boondocking life. She might never know the beautiful joy of holding her baby like Kenzie was now or like Lauren would soon. There was no denying the hurt in that. But God held her there, gently. Faithfully.

Lovingly. *Remind me again, Lord, when the pain is acute. Remind me ever again.*

She reached into the box of mail that Jacob had left on the captain's seat and withdrew an opened envelope. "Jacob just opened a letter from Yellowstone this morning—he landed a seasonal job at the park. Groundskeeper. We'll head that way next week and stay through August. Then he's got a lead for a beet-harvesting job up in Montana in the fall. After that we'll likely head back to the Coachella Valley for the beginning of the orange harvest. The owners of Salazar Farms, where Jacob worked this spring, have promised him a job. Hopefully, we'll get to see some other national parks in between all of that, and we'd like to find time to stop at Bryce and Sally's—the people who helped us at the beginning—after their baby is born." Anticipation seeped through Kate while she shared their tentative plans.

Pure joy rippled through Helen's laugh as she stood and hugged Kate. "You're on quite a journey, my love. I can't wait to read all about it."

Kate amended her newfound definition of luxury. Being loved and forgiven—as Helen was showing her in that moment—made it onto that list. She felt strength rising in her spirit, lifted by that love and by gratitude.

This life was an adventure, one full of ups and downs. Of laughter and joy, of tears and heartache. But not an empty one, and certainly not a hopeless one. It was a life she'd never dreamed of, and that seemed like quite a surprise. Kate, the fabricator of a great lie and the writer of many stories, was, after all, a pretty big dreamer.

God had shown Himself to be bigger. And, she'd found, His dreams for her were so much better than hers ever could be.

ThisBoondockingLife entry #53

So now you know the story, and Jake and I have nearly come full circle. We've been living this boondocking life for eight months now, and wow! It's been something. The pictures I've posted are woefully insufficient. The places we've seen, the sights we've beheld! Sunsets over the Tetons, late-summers snow in Yellowstone. The deep and dangerous pools of steaming water, beautiful with their gem coloring. The spray of Old Faithful. The thunderous falls. And then there was the jaw-dropping enormity of Glacier National Park. I can't wait to go back and explore more, as we only scratched the surface.

For now, we travel south again. This week, we visit the parks in Utah. Once again, Jake and I are awestruck by the unique beauty. Zion, Bryce, Arches, Canyonlands...

Stunning. Simply stunning.

And I haven't even started with the things we've learned about ourselves, about each other, and most importantly, about God.

Turns out, my first friend in the boondocking life had been right—what I thought had been the worst thing ever turned out to be the greatest blessing.

Jake and me—we love this life.

Chapter Twenty-Two
(in which they are thankful)

Kate leaned against Jacob's shoulder, mesmerized by the view stretching beneath their dangling feet. Despite the heavy chill and dark-gray clouds, they'd bundled into their warm hiking gear and taken to the trail they'd chosen in the Needles District, trusting that the forecast would be accurate and the weather would clear. The trail had been worth the shivers, and the sunrise over the painted walls of predominately red sandstone worth their early morning.

The storm across the canyon broke apart, dark-gray clouds giving way to wispy white ones, which also yielded to the light-blue sky. Oddly, the view reminded her of that one awful night back in Seattle—the one where she'd intended to tell Jacob that she was leaving. They'd flung horrible accusations at each other during that fight—she, that he'd only married her to get back at Jackson. He, that she'd taken up with him because he was a safer financial bet.

That had been quite a storm between them. And yet looking back on it now, it had also been the break in their relationship. The one they needed, painful though it was. So much like what she was seeing play out against the colorful cliff walls in that moment. The cleansing, the clearing.

New hope.

"I loved you from the beginning," she whispered, gripping his bicep as her head remained on his shoulder. "I want you to know that, Jacob. I need you to know that."

Jacob shifted so that he could wrap his arms around her. His hold was firm and warm. Resolute and determined. So very much the man she'd fallen in love with. The one that, despite everything, she still loved. Now more than ever.

His lips pressed against her hat, warm breath seeping through the knitted garment. "I loved you too. I have always loved you, Katie. No matter what life looks like, I will always love you."

Kate shut her eyes and pressed into him, pure, overwhelming beauty in her heart. Utter amazement engulfed her, pricking tears behind her closed lids. *Thank You.*

As if he'd heard her silent prayer, Jacob's embrace pressed her in closer, and he tipped his chin skyward. "Thank You, Lord of heaven and earth. Thank You for *this* life. No matter what it looks like now or in the future—a skoolie, a trailer, a condo, a house— we're grateful for this life You've given us, and we chose to worship You in it."

Amen and amen.

The miracles, they just kept coming.

The end.

We meet here at the end again, my friends. This was quite a journey for me—I hope it was a beautiful one for you. My prayer is always that these stories will inspire my readers to worship. While *This Life* is a work of fiction, God's goodness certainly is not.

Would you do me the honor of leaving a review for *This Life*? Simply go to Amazon (or Goodreads), and share what you thought with other readers.

The Murphy Brothers Stories will continue with *Stubborn Love.* Tyler Murphy had his own tough mountains to climb, and I hope you'll want to come along that trail with him. *Stubborn Love* will release in May 2021, and you can preorder your copy now.

As always, thank you so much for reading! I'm honored that you'd give me your time.

Jen